Entertaining on the Jewish Holidays

ENTERTAINING ON THE JEWISH HOLIDAYS

Israela Banin

A division of Shapolsky Publishers, Inc.

S.P.I. BOOKS

A division of Shapolsky Publishers, Inc.

For any additional information, contact:

S.P.I Books / Shapolsky Publishers, Inc.
136 West 22nd Street
New York, NY 10011
212/633-2022   FAX 212/633-2123

10 9 8 7 6 5 4 3 2 1

ISBN 1056171-018-0

Library of Congress Cataloging-in-Publication Data

Banin, Israela, 19-
    Entertaining on the Jewish Holidays   Israela Banin.
        p.   cm.
    ISBN 1-56171-018-0
    1. Cookery, Jewish   2. Holiday cookery.   I. Title.
TX724.B26   1991
641.5'676 – dc20

Design and Typography by Smith, Inc., New York
Printed in Canada

*With love, to my husband, Ram — for his
support and good nature*

Centerpiece for a Rosh Hashanah table

CONTENTS

PREFACE

My essential purpose in writing this book was to make it as easy as possible for busy people to celebrate the Sabbath and Jewish holidays by inviting family and friends over for dinner. For each celebration, therefore, I've suggested meals that can be prepared without too much trouble. Most of the recipes I've provided are quite simple, and many of the dishes can be prepared in advance. All the dishes can be made in accordance with kosher laws, if desired.

Similarly, for the table decorations I've focused on centerpieces and ornaments that can be found around the house or purchased inexpensively at neighborhood stores. The same linens and set of dishes can be used for every occasion, although I do make suggestions for alternative table coverings and napkins.

For those who are not familiar with the ceremonies, I've included brief explanations of the required ceremonial objects and foods. But I've omitted descriptions of the ceremonies themselves. Excellent instructional books are already available.

Since it's customary for guests to give their hosts gifts, I've included suggestions for inexpensive ones. In addition, I've provided ideas for presents to give guests as mementos of the occasion.

I'd like to express my deep gratitude to the friends who have generously helped me in the preparation of the book.

Special thanks to Sara Freeman and Rena Pascal for taking the time to read and discuss the manuscript. Their comments and moral support were invaluable.

The rich variety of recipes for the various Jewish holidays was made possible by contributions from Dalia Freeman, Sara Freeman, Adit Gozani, Linda Gross, Lorrie Lewis, Orna Makleff, Nitza Manna, Rena Pascal, Miriam Resnick, and Yvette Resnick.

Table decorations were greatly enhanced by the loan of ceremonial objects from the exceptional Judaica collection of Adele Lieberman, and by beautiful Judaica ornaments lent by Nurit Levanon and Daniela Smith. Other outstanding artifacts and ornaments were lent by Bob and Bob Fine Jewish Gifts, Crafts, and Books (Palo Alto, California) and by California Craft & Floral (also of Palo Alto).

Cantor Hans Cohen made a very important contribution to the book by helping me locate and select appropriate songs for the holidays.

Many thanks to all of you. I am very privileged to have such friends.

I am particularly grateful to Dr. Robert Abramson, Director of the Education Department of the United Synagogue of America, for granting me permission to reproduce selected words and music from Harry Coopersmith's book *More of the Songs We Sing* (New York: United Synagogue of America, 1971).

In addition, I want to thank my family: my husband Ram, who has been supportive and understanding and has provided helpful advice throughout the project; my children Anat and Yoav, who survived the ordeal without complaining. Yoav even edited and typed the manuscript.

The photographs are by Vano Photography (San Francisco), and editorial assistance was provided by Editorial Consultants, Inc. (San Francisco). My thanks to them, too, for their contributions.

Israela Banin
Palo Alto, California,
1991

CHAPTER 1

INTRODUCTION:
Entertaining Made Easy

The Lord appeared to [Abraham] by the terebinths of Mamre; he was sitting at the entrance of the tent as the day grew hot. Looking up, he saw three men standing near him. As soon as he saw them, he ran from the entrance of the tent to greet them and, bowing to the ground, he said, "My lords, if it please you, do not go on past your servant. Let a little water be brought; bathe your feet and recline under the tree. And let me fetch a morsel of bread that you may refresh yourselves; then go on—seeing that you have come your servant's way." They replied, "Do as you have said."

Abraham hastened into the tent to Sarah, and said, "Quick, three measures of choice flour! Knead and make cakes!" Then Abraham ran to the herd, took a calf, tender and choice, and gave it to the servant, who hastened to prepare it. He took curds and milk and the calf that had been prepared, and set these before them; and he waited on them under the tree as they ate.

Genesis 18:1-8

Ever since the destruction of the Second Temple by the Romans, observance of the Sabbath and Jewish holidays has centered on family gatherings around the dinner table. As the Talmud says, the table has become the temple. The ceremonies we perform at home on Friday nights and festivals are usually accompanied by sumptuous meals served on our best dishes. Often we invite friends to join us in keeping with the Jewish tradition of hospitality. Even the somber High Holy Days involve the preparation of food and some entertaining, although subdued.

You don't have to be religious to celebrate the Sabbath and holidays. Many families set aside Friday nights as a time to get together with each other and friends after a busy week. It's a secular way of maintaining the traditional Sabbath observance and thereby reaffirming our Jewish identity. Most of the holidays commemorate events in Jewish history. When we celebrate them, we are reminded of our unique heritage and culture. While the ceremonies performed have deep religious meaning, of course, they are also occasions for social gatherings.

What all this comes down to in practice is that the gatherings are dinner parties. Whether the party is an intimate one for the immediate family or a gala, it involves the preparation of food, decoration of the table, and selection of ceremonial objects. The purpose of this book is to make it as easy as possible to serve appropriate meals and create an atmosphere that truly reflects the spirit of the observance. For the Sabbath and each holiday, the book includes suggested menus with recipes, ideas for table decorations, and explanations of required ceremonial objects. Since it's customary for a guest to bring a present for the host, a list of suitable gifts is also included.

Delicious Meals

Traditionally, the main way we Jews offer hospitality is with food. And we serve it in abundance. However, generosity must not be overwhelming. The food should not be so costly or exotic that a guest would be made to feel inferior or unable to reciprocate. Certain dishes have therefore become more or less standard fare because they are, or at least used to be, relatively inexpensive. In central and eastern Europe, hence also the United States, pot roast, chicken, kreplach, and gefilte fish are typical favorites. But they can be made in many different ways, and there are numerous other dishes that are just as suitable. The recipes in this book include variations on old standbys and suggestions for alternative dishes. They have been selected with a view to simplifying the preparation of delicious meals.

Dramatic Table Decoration

One of the major opportunities for expressing the spirit of a holiday is, unfortunately, often neglected. The usual practice is to set the table with the finest linens and best dinnerware, glasses, and silverware, along with the requisite ceremonial objects. The centerpiece might consist of candles (almost always required) and flowers or a plant. Such a table is nice enough and can be quite elegant. But the decoration is just about the same for all the holidays. A reflection of the distinctive meaning of the celebration is lacking.

The key to the art of table decoration is symbolism. Colors and decorative elements should represent the story and spirit of the holiday. On Purim, for example, black triangular place mats (easily cut out of crepe or gift paper) symbolize Haman's three-cornered hat. A few bricks placed on the Passover table, perhaps for use as trivets or to form a base for the seder plate, remind us of the role played by our ancestors in building Egyptian tombs. Dramatic, original, and beautiful table decorations can be created inexpensively and easily with items found around the house or available at variety, paper-goods, and other stores.

Artistic Ceremonial Objects

The designs of Jewish ceremonial objects are as varied as the cultures of the nations in which Jews have lived, as the styles of changing times, and as the creativity of individual craftsmen. We therefore have a great deal of latitude in regard to whether the style of the object is traditional or contemporary, how it is decorated, and which material it's made out of. Naturally, the design must be functional and in good taste.*

---

*For a treasury of information about the design of Jewish ceremonial objects, see Abram Kanof, *Jewish Ceremonial Art and Religious Observance* (New York: Harry N. Abrams, Inc., Publishers, n.d.).

Since the lighting of candles begins and ends the Sabbath and is customary on most holidays, candle holders are basic ceremonial objects and consequently prominent elements in almost every table decoration. Collecting candle holders can be a fascinating and very practical hobby. A well-rounded collection would include a variety of traditional and modern designs so that appropriate holders are at hand for whatever type of table setting is selected for a celebration. Oil lamps—like those used in Biblical times and the Middle Ages—might be substituted for candles on some occasions. An oil lamp consists essentially of a small receptacle containing olive or vegetable oil in which a wick is floated. (For instructions on how to make lamps out of baby-food jars and other containers available at home, see Chapter 5.)

Another basic object is the kiddush cup. Any goblet can be used for reciting kiddush as long as its rim is not flawed. Although usually cylindrical, a cup might be hexagonal or octagonal or square, might or might not have a stem, might be absolutely plain or elaborately decorated, and can be made out of metal, glass, wood, or conceivably even plastic. Decoration ordinarily consists of religious symbols or scenes, but secular motifs are acceptable. Inscribed biblical quotations are popular. If a family has different cups for various occasions—one for the Sabbath, another for Passover, perhaps others for Shavuoth and Sukkoth—inscriptions might indicate when the cup is to be used: for example, "Remember the Sabbath day and keep it holy," or "For the Holy Sabbath." But poetry, or a dedication if the cup is a gift, will do just as well.

Practical Gifts

The rule about not serving expensive foods applies to the selection of a gift for the host. It should not be so costly or exquisite that the host would have trouble reciprocating. Be careful about the old standbys wine and flowers. They're not always appropriate.

An Enriching Experience

Entertaining on a holiday can be a profoundly enriching experience. In preparing the meal and decorating the table, we approach the holiday creatively. We express our own perception of the celebration and thereby deepen our spiritual and moral understanding of its significance. Every time we entertain we learn something new about our heritage—and about ourselves as Jews. A celebration thus becomes a quest for knowledge, and the Talmud teaches us that knowledge is the true path to personal satisfaction.

CHAPTER 2
The Sabbath

You shall remember that you were a servant in the land of Egypt, and the Lord your God brought you out thence by a mighty hand and by an outstretched arm; therefore the Lord your God commanded you to keep the sabbath day.

Deuteronomy 5:15

In the ghettos of Europe, preparation for the Sabbath used to begin early Friday morning with the lighting of the ovens. The crowded food stores and pervasive aroma of cooking created a festive atmosphere which mounted steadily during the day until mid-afternoon, when the fires were extinguished, families changed into their best clothes, and the men left for the synagogue. A stillness would descend upon the community. When the men returned from the synagogue, they would often bring a guest for dinner, preferably a Talmudic student who would edify their families with pious conversation.

The drama can still be found in some of Israel's traditionalist communities, particularly in sections of Jerusalem, where the approaching Sabbath is announced in the same way it was in the days of the Temple. On Friday afternoon loud blasts of the shofar advise the populace that it's time to get ready. With another clarion later on, the shops close. Just before sundown the shofar announces the arrival of the Sabbath—it is time to light the candles.

The Sabbath is the most important celebration in the Jewish calendar. Instituted by the Fourth Commandment, it is a weekly reminder of the gift of creation. In addition, it commemorates our liberation from slavery and the establishment of Jewish nationhood. The Sabbath thus stands for our freedom as a people.

For mankind in general the commandment to observe the Sabbath has had a more beneficent influence than almost any other precept in religious history. Every country in the world now accepts the principle that its citizens are entitled to at least one day a week off from work.

The spirit of the celebration was captured exquisitely by the mystic Cabalists of the sixteenth century, who personified the Sabbath as the royal bride of Israel. Just before sundown Friday nights they would walk in a procession to the edge of town to greet the bride, singing psalms as they went. The ceremony is still performed symbolically in the synagogue Friday evenings when we face the door to greet the Sabbath.

When we entertain, we should try to create a feeling of deep satisfaction with the arrival of a loved one, whose presence among us is an occasion for great rejoicing but whose departure is imminent. Our goal must be warmth and beauty. We serve sumptuous meals, especially Friday night, and use our finest tableware. For table decorations, appropriate colors are white, cream, silver (all representing purity), blue (love of divine works), gold (good fortune), yellow (wisdom), and purple (royalty—the bride of Israel).

Because the Sabbath is fundamental to Jewish life, it deserves the very best we have to offer.

SPECIAL SABBATH FOODS

Three meals are supposed to be eaten on the Sabbath – an indication of just how important food is in Jewish ceremony. The main one, of course, is Friday night dinner, although there was some controversy in the Talmud about whether it should be included. Breakfast the next morning, however light, and a midday lunch or dinner are the others. In addition, dinner or supper is eaten after sundown with the Habdalah, the ceremony that marks the departure of the Sabbath. While there are no rules about what foods should be served, except for wine and bread, certain dishes are traditional:

CHALLAH. The Sabbath bread may be baked in any shape, but since the Middle Ages the dough has been twisted or braided into the familiar loaf found in Jewish bakeries throughout the Western world. Two loaves must be served. They represent the double portion of manna given the Israelites during their wandering in the desert so that they would not have to gather food on the Sabbath. During the kiddush the bread is covered with a special cloth in commemoration of the dew that lay on the manna and to make the point that the loaves are not merely for the purpose of satisfying hunger. A piece of the challah is broken or sliced off for the kiddush blessing and shared by everyone at the table. In many homes the piece of bread is sprinkled with salt after the blessing to remind us that we must earn the bread we eat by the sweat of our brows.

GEFILTE FISH. A deliciously spicy mixture of fish, egg, and other ingredients is stuffed into a fish (hence the name of the dish) or made into balls or cakes and boiled. Fish has been a favorite Sabbath dish since the Middle Ages, and the rabbis appropriately have found meaning in the pleasure. We eat fish, they say, to remind ourselves that just as it cannot live outside water, we Jews cannot survive without the Torah.

CHICKEN SOUP. The widely spread belief in the medicinal benefits of chicken soup has been shown to have a foundation in fact. But its popularity as a Sabbath dish is probably based on economics: soup is filling, especially if fortified with noodles, and after it's made the bird can be removed and served as a separate dish.

CHOLENT. A combination of meat and a variety of vegetables, which are all baked together slowly, the cholent is cooked on Friday for consumption on Saturday. The dish probably originated in the Rhineland in the early Middle Ages.

KUGEL. If part of the Friday night dinner, this pudding-like dish made of noodles or potatoes is served on a round plate to symbolize the weekly Sabbath-to-Sabbath cycle. Usually, however, Kugel is eaten on Saturday.

WINE. The kiddush cup is filled with sweet red wine, symbolizing the sweetness of the Sabbath.

FRIDAY NIGHT DINNER

Elegance is the key word for the Friday night dinner. We usually set the table with our best linens, silverware, glassware, and candlesticks. But this does not mean that the table must be staid and dull. Colorfulness is very much in keeping with the affirmative spirit of the Sabbath. The meal is usually very large and includes appetizer, soup, a hearty main dish, vegetables, and dessert. Some families establish their own Sabbath tradition by serving the same dishes every Friday night.

CEREMONIAL OBJECTS

CANDLES. At least two. Some families add an additional one for each child. Others light seven, one for each day of the week; or ten, one for each commandment.

KIDDUSH CUP. The cup should be large. If everyone at the table recites the kiddush, any cups or goblets may be used as long as they do not have handles and the rims are unflawed.

CHALLAH COVER. The cloth should be large enough to completely cover two loaves of challah—about 12x18 inches. A good napkin may be used. But many families have special embroidered covers made of linen or other fine material.

MENU

> *Gefilte fish*
> *Chicken noodle soup*
> *Brisket of beef with wine and olives*
> *Rice*
> *Green salad*
> *Relish—olives, celery, radishes*
> *Fresh fruit cup, flavored with sweet red wine*

TABLE DECORATION

For a traditional table setting, use blue or white linens and candles. Place the candlesticks in the middle of the table. If two are used, put a vase of colorful flowers or a plant between them. (Lacking flowers or a plant, use a bowl of fruit.) If there are more candlesticks, intersperse them with individual flowers and border the line of candles with fern or green leaves. Place the kiddush cup and decanter of wine to the right of the place setting of the person reciting the kiddush. The challah should be nearby for the breaking of the bread. To add sparkle to the table, place flowers on the napkins—or, if possible, wrap the stems around the napkins as if they were napkin rings.

Colorful alternative ideas for decorating the table include use of:

- Centerpiece consisting of a queen doll surrounded by candles. (For the queen, you can use any doll dressed in white, but make a little veil out of cheese cloth or a piece of lace.)

- Napkin rings shaped like crowns. (If you can't find them in a store, cut serrated strips out of gold gift paper and paste the ends together.)

- Small vase of flowers at each place setting.

- Yellow or gold tablecloth, with navy-blue napkins. For the centerpiece, use blue and white candles. Spread flowers and leaves around the table to create the feeling of a park. Amid them place miniature bridal veils and men's hats (symbolizing the royal bride and Israelite groom.)

- Different candle holders, perhaps a collection, lined up the length of the table as a centerpiece.

- Garland (the ancient form of crown) made out of flowers, representing the royal bride Sabbath, placed between the two candlesticks.

- Napkin rings made of white paper on which the words "Shabbat Shalom" are written with the names of the guests.

- A candle at each place setting, with a miniature Torah next to it.

- Toy animals (or figurines) on or next to the children's plates, representing the Fourth Commandment's enjoinder that animals, as well as humans, should have a day of rest.

SUMMARY OF SUGGESTED ORNAMENTS

Animals (toys or figurines)
Bridal veils and men's hats
Candle-holder collection
Flowers
Garland(s)
Leaves
Napkin rings shaped like crowns, or made out of white paper and inscribed
    with names of guests and words "Shabbat Shalom"
Plant
Queen Doll

SATURDAY LUNCHEON

Cholent is the customary main dish for the Saturday midday meal and a superb selection, especially if prepared the day before, because the flavors of the meat and vegetables will have had a chance to blend. Raisins and nuts, either as a relish or dessert, are traditional European Sabbath refreshments. Even if the candles lit Friday have burned out, the candle holders should remain on the table. No new candles are lit, of course. It is not necessary to use wine for the kiddush. Any beverage will do. The challah is not covered.

MENU

> *Broiled grapefruit*
> *Cholent*
> *Salad*
> *Challah*
> *Raisins and nuts*
> *Sorbet or non-dairy sherbet*

TABLE DECORATION

The tablecloth and decoration used for Friday night dinner are often kept on the table Saturday. But the custom of taking a walk Saturday afternoon might be represented by a doll couple (perhaps holding hands) as a centerpiece and flowers and leaves strewn around the table. Cut the stems off the flowers.

HABDALAH

Symbolically, the Habdalah ceremony separates the spirituality of the Sabbath from the crassness of the rest of the week. It is therefore tinged with sadness. To relieve the gloom, a box of spices is passed around the table and the fragrance inhaled after the blessing of the wine. Then special braided candles are lit. Some wine is spilled from the kiddush cup to express the hope that blessings will overflow during the coming week, which is formally inaugurated by extinguishing the candles in the spilled wine. After the heavy Friday night dinner and Saturday luncheon, a dairy supper is often welcome.

CEREMONIAL OBJECTS

CANDLES.   Long and braided, preferably with two or more wicks.

KIDDUSH CUP.   Provide a saucer in which to spill the wine.

SPICES.   Cloves, cinnamon, fresh marjoram, rosemary, and dried oregano are especially suitable. They have very pleasant aromas and are available in almost every grocery.

SPICE BOX.   Any small box will do, but it should be as lovely as possible and must have a cover.

MENU

> *Gefilte fish*
> *Cheese blintzes*
> *Vegetable salad*
> *Challah or other bread*
> *Strudel or fresh fruit*

TABLE DECORATION

Use a white or blue tablecloth and napkins. Down the center of the table place the symbols of the evening—two candle holders with the braided Habdalah candles in the middle, the kiddush cup or cups, and the spice box. Between them, place individual flowers and leaves. To enliven the table, scatter golden paper stars around the tablecloth. Next to each guest, place a perfume bottle. If the bottles are empty, put small aromatic flowers in them.

GIFTS FOR THE HOST
(Dinner, Luncheon, or Habdalah)

Book about the Sabbath
Cake
Candle holder
Candles, particularly special ones for Habdalah
Challah cover
Challah knife
Coaster for kiddush cup
Fruit
Plant
Sabbath stories for children
Special saucer for the kiddush cup on Habdalah
Spice box
Spices
Sweet red wine

MEMENTOS FOR GUESTS
(Dinner, Luncheon, or Habdalah)

Challah roll
Chocolate kisses wrapped in cheese cloth (to simulate veils)
Flower, with its stem wrapped in tissue paper
Paper coasters, shaped like birds or Stars of David
Place card or napkin ring, inscribed with guest's name and
     words "Shabbat Shalom"

CHECK LIST OF SABBATH BASICS

Challah, two loaves
Red wine
Spices
Candle holders, at least two
Candles, plain for Friday night
Candles, long and braided, with two or more wicks for
     Habdalah

Kiddush cup
Challah cover
Kipots (yarmulkes)
Flowers or plant (yellow)

RECIPES

GEFILTE FISH

(Simple Method)   Serves 6

*1 whole carp, pike, or similar freshwater fish skinned and
  fileted, or 3 lbs. frozen filets thawed
3 medium-size onions
1 slice of bread, soaked in water and squeezed dry
2 eggs
3 tbsp. bread crumbs
2 tbsp. sugar
1/2 tsp. salt
1/2 tsp. black pepper*

Cut the fish filets into slices, and grind with onions and the slice of moistened bread. Add eggs and bread crumbs, and grind again. Place mixture in a big bowl, and add sugar, salt, and pepper. Mix ingredients thoroughly and form into oval patties. (To make it easier to form patties, put a little vegetable oil on hands.) Drop patties gently into boiling water. Reduce heat and simmer about two hours. Serve at room temperature or cold.

GEFILTE FISH

(Traditional Method)   Serves 8 or more

*3-4 lbs. yellow or blue pike, whitefish mullet, and snapper or bream
  (Use at least two, preferably three, kinds of fish.)
2 eggs
2 or 3 medium-size onions
1/2 cup matzo meal
Tops from 1 bunch of celery, chopped
2 or 3 medium-size carrots, peeled and sliced
Salt and pepper to taste*

Clean, skin, and bone the fish, preserving bones and keeping the skin as whole as possible. Cut the fish into small pieces and grind or chop it with the onion. Put aside two or three onion slices, separated into rings. Add the eggs, matzo meal, salt, and pepper, and mix well. Rinse fish skins and cut into wide strips. Oil hands slightly with vegetable oil, roll mixture into oval balls and wrap each one in a piece of fish skin. Put celery tops, onion rings, carrots, and fish bones into water, bring to boil, and lower fish balls gently into water with slotted ladle. Reduce heat and simmer for about an hour, making sure that water level is always above the fish balls. Serve at room temperature or cold, with beet horseradish.

CHICKEN SOUP

Serves 8

3-4 lb. chicken, cut up (without liver)
1 1/2 onions, sliced
6 small carrots peeled and cut into chunks
1/4 bunch celery, sliced (with or without leaves)
1 green pepper, halved
2 zucchini
2 parsnips (optional)
1 bay leaf
1/2 tsp. minced garlic
Salt and black pepper to taste
Water, enough to just cover the chicken

Put chicken into large pot with water, bring to boil with pot partly covered. Reduce heat, skim fat from surface of water, and add rest of ingredients. Cover pot and simmer for 1 1/2 hours. Put through strainer and throw out the vegetables. Add cooked noodles or other pasta to broth, if desired, and cook for eight more minutes. (Broth can be kept in freezer for a month or longer.)

BRISKET WITH WINE AND OLIVES

Serves 6-8

3-lb. brisket of beef
5 cloves garlic, minced
4-oz. can black olives, pitted
1/4 lb. carrots, cut into cubes
2 stalks celery, sliced
1 green pepper, sliced
5 large tomatoes, cut into quarters
4 onions, sliced
1 cup dry red wine
5 tbsp. olive oil
1 tbsp. parsley, chopped
1 tsp. dried dill, or 2 tsp. fresh
Salt and pepper to taste

Heat olive oil in large skillet. Saute onions, carrots, celery, and green pepper for a few minutes. Do not brown. Add wine, salt, pepper, garlic, and spices. Cook for a few minutes, then allow to cool and pour over meat. Cover tightly and marinate meat in refrigerator overnight, turning two or three times if possible. Put meat and marinade into a large covered pot, and simmer for 1 1/2 hours or until almost done. Add tomatoes and olives, then cook until very tender.

CHOLENT

Serves 6-8

3 lbs. beef brisket or boneless chuck
1 lb. small lima beans, washed and drained
4 medium-size carrots, cut in half
2 medium onions, cut in thin slices
2 tbsp. flour
3 lbs. potatoes, sliced crosswise approximately 1/2- to 1-
inch pieces
1/2 tsp. paprika
salt and pepper to taste

Mix all ingredients except the meat and place in a casserole or a large oven-proof pot. Place meat on top of the mixture, cover with water, and bring to a boil, then reduce heat and simmer for 20 minutes. Preheat oven to 225 degrees. Cover pot or casserole tightly and bake overnight. Do not turn oven off until after the Sabbath.

CHOLENT

(Northeastern Style)   Serves 4-6

1 cup white beans
1 cup garbanzo beans
2 large onions, sliced
8 large potatoes, peeled (leave whole)
1 whole garlic head
1/4 tsp. pepper
1/2 tsp. salt
2 cups water
8 fresh eggs, hard-boiled

Soak white and garbanzo beans overnight, then drain. (Canned beans may be used, but discard liquid before adding to other ingredients.) Place all ingredients except eggs in a large roasting pan or casserole, bring to boil, then reduce heat and simmer overnight. Before serving add hard-boiled, unshelled eggs.

CHEESE BLINTZES
(Israeli Style. For another recipe, see Chapter 5, Hanukkah.)

Serves 4-8

Filling
4 cups cream-style cottage cheese
4 tbsp. sour cream
2 egg yolks
3 tbsp. sugar
1/2 tbsp. salt
1 tbsp. vanilla (optional)

Mix all the ingredients, and set aside.

Dough
2 large eggs
3/4 cup milk
1/2-2/3 cup flour, sifted
pinch of salt
2 tbsp. margarine, melted
Vegetable oil or margarine for frying

Mix the eggs and milk until well blended. Add flour, salt, and melted margarine, and whip mixture until smooth. Spread a thin layer of margarine and oil in an 8-inch frying pan. Pour in two tbsp. of batter, tilting pan to spread batter evenly. Cook over medium heat until batter bubbles and begins to thicken on top into a crepe-like consistency. Place dough bottom side up on wax paper or cloth, and allow to cool. Spoon out one or two tablespoons of the filling, and spread evenly along the middle. Starting at one edge, roll the pancake around the filling.

Repeat procedures for making and rolling dough until the filling is used up. Add margarine and oil to the pan and heat until it is bubbling, but not smoking, and fry the blintzes until they're golden brown. Then place blintzes in a single layer on a lightly greased baking pan, and allow them to cool. Cover pan tightly, and refrigerate blintzes overnight. Reheat from room temperature in 325 degree oven. Serve with topping of sour cream, powdered sugar, honey, apple sauce, or fresh or frozen berries.

KUGEL

(Dairy Version)   Serves 4

2 cups milk
2 eggs
1 lb. medium-size flat noodles
1/4 cup raisins
1/4 cup chopped or slivered almonds, unsalted
1/2 cup granulated sugar
1 tbsp. powdered sugar
Ground cinnamon to taste
1 tsp. salt

Boil noodles until al dente, rinse in hot water, drain, and set aside. Mix milk, eggs, raisins, almonds, granulated sugar, and salt. Add cooked noodles, and stir until well mixed. Pour mixture into well-greased 9x13-inch baking pan. Preheat oven to 350 degrees and bake until golden brown (30–45 minutes). Remove from oven, and sprinkle with powdered sugar mixed with cinnamon. May be served hot or cold.

STRUDEL

Serves 8 or more

Dough
2 cups flour
One 8-oz. package of cream cheese
2 sticks butter or margarine

Filling
2 cups apricot jam
2 cups chopped walnuts
1 cup yellow raisins
2 tbsp. powdered sugar

Mix the flour, cream cheese, and butter or margarine into a smooth and pliable paste. Refrigerate for a few hours or overnight. Divide dough into four equal parts and roll each out into a thin 9x13-inch rectangle. Mix jam, walnuts, and raisins, and spread one-fourth of mixture on each piece of dough. Starting from the edge, roll the dough around the filling, and place the rolls in a single layer on a greased cookie sheet. Cut slits about one inch apart into tops of rolls. Preheat oven to 350 degrees and bake until golden brown (40–60 minutes). Allow to cool for 5 or 10 minutes. Sprinkle powdered sugar on top, and slice each roll into six to eight pieces.

BROILED GRAPEFRUIT

Serves 6

3 grapefruit
1/2 cup honey or brown sugar
6 maraschino cherries

Cut grapefruit in half crosswise. Separate pulp from skin by cutting carefully along edge of pulp. (Special curved and serrated knives are available for this—they make the task much easier.) Make sure that the bitter white lining of the skin is not attached to the pulp. Core out the white center of the grapefruit, and carefully separate the fruit segments into bite-size pieces (usually two segments). Spread honey or brown sugar on top of halves. Broil, with fruit about six inches away from flame or heating element, until top begins to turn brown. Place maraschino cherry in the hole formed by coring out the center.

CHAPTER 3

Rosh Hashanah
(Tishri 1–2: September or October)
and
Yom Kippur
(Tishri 10: September or October)

*And the Lord spoke to Moses, saying: Speak to the children of Israel, saying,
In the seventh month, in the first day of the month, you shall have a solemn
rest, a memorial proclaimed with the blast of horns, a holy convocation.*

Leviticus 23:23-24

According to Jewish lore, God has a book of life which is divided into three sections: one for righteous Jews, another for the wicked, and the third for those who are somewhere between. At the blast of the shofar on Rosh Hashanah, God opens the book and in the first section inscribes the names of the righteous, awarding them a good life during the coming year. In the second, He enters the names of the wicked, and they are condemned to a miserable year or death. The rest, whose names He writes in the third section, have until Yom Kippur to repent.

Rosh Hashanah and Yom Kippur are unlike any other holidays in the Jewish calendar. They do not commemorate events in our history or glorify nature, although some Talmudists contend that Rosh Hashanah is the anniversary of the creation. We do not celebrate them with festivities, as we do other holidays. Instead we devote ourselves to introspection, penitence, and atonement, to examination of our relationship with God and our fellow men. The solemnity of the observances is represented by the Hebrew name of the ten-day period from Rosh Hashanah to Yom Kippur, Yamim Mor'im—the Days of Awe. In English-speaking countries, particularly the United States, the period is known as the High Holy Days or High Holidays.

While the Torah instructs us to observe the first day of the seventh month (Tishri) as a memorial, the Bible never refers to the holiday as Rosh Hashanah—that is, New Year's Day. In Numbers 29:1 it is called Day of Blowing the Shofar (Yom Trua). The name Rosh Hashanah does not appear in Jewish literature until after the destruction of the Second Temple. By then, however, the identification of Tishri 1 with the beginning of the year was probably well-established. Sometimes the holiday is referred to as the Day of Memorial (Yom Hazikkaron) or as the Day of Judgment (Yom Hadin) when God evaluates our deeds of the previous year.

19

Rosh Hashanah is the only holiday that is observed for two days in Israel, as well as in the Diaspora. The custom arose because in the days before scientific calendars it was difficult to determine precisely when the new moon arrived marking the first day of a month (rosh hodesh). Commencement of a new month therefore did not become official until the central court (beth din) in Jerusalem had accepted testimony from two witnesses that they had seen the new moon with their own eyes. All this took time, so it was sometimes necessary to extend the Tishri 1 observance to two days. After the destruction of the Second Temple, the second day was discontinued in the Holy Land, but then it was resumed during the Middle Ages in commemoration of the Temple.

The extra day added to the celebration of holidays in the Diaspora has a different, although not unrelated, origin. Since only the central beth din had the authority to determine when a month began and the dates of festivals, outlying Jewish communities depended on messages from Jerusalem for the information. At first a system of lighting hilltop beacons was employed. It was so efficient that the message reached as far away as Egypt and Babylonia in a matter of hours. But the Samaritans sabotaged the system, and it was replaced by the slower method of dispatching messengers. To allow time for them to arrive, the Sukkoth, Passover, and Shavuoth festivals were extended by a day. This "second holiday of the Diaspora" was not added to Yom Kippur because of the hardship of fasting for more than twenty-four hours.

Rosh Hashanah is symbolized by the shofar, its plaintive sound reflecting perfectly the spirit of the holiday. The philosopher Maimonides wrote: "The Scriptural injunction of the shofar for New Year's Day has a profound meaning. It says: Awake, ye sleepers, and ponder your Creator and go back to Him in penitence. Be not of those who miss realities in the pursuit of shadows and waste their years in seeking after vain things which cannot profit or deliver. Look well to your souls and consider your acts; forsake each of you his evil ways and thoughts, and return to God so that He may have mercy upon you." To prepare us for Rosh Hashanah and Yom Kippur, the shofar is sounded during morning prayers throughout the preceding month, Elul. It is a meritorious act to hear, but not to blow, the shofar. (Note that the shofar is not sounded on the Sabbath.) Ordinarily, the instrument is made out of a ram's horn and is thus reminiscent of the animal God gave Abraham to sacrifice in place of Isaac. But the horn of any split-hoofed animal may be used, except cattle because of their association with worship of the golden calf.

Although Rosh Hashanah does not focus as much as other holidays on ceremonies held at the dinner table, it is customary for relatives and friends to call upon one another around the time of the holiday to exchange greetings. Inviting loved ones for dinner is a great way to express our wishes for a Happy New Year. For those who drop in to wish us *shanah tovah,* a good year, we might prepare a welcoming dessert table with coffee, tea, and cake. On the afternoon of Rosh Hashanah we might invite our guests to accompany us on a walk to a nearby river or other flowing body of water to perform the traditional ceremony of the tashlik (from the Hebrew word meaning to cast away). While reciting penitential prayers and verses from Micah, we throw bread crumbs into the water or shake our clothes to signify our desire to cast our sins into the depths of the sea where they will be washed away.

The spirit of renewal and purification is also expressed by the custom of buying new clothes for Rosh Hashanah. Some families wear white, just as the rabbis and cantors don a white robe called a kittel during the Days of Awe in memory of the high priest of

Jerusalem who wore a similar garment in the Temple. In addition to representing purity, white serves as a reminder of our mortality, since that is the color of the burial shroud. Among traditionalists it is also customary to wear cloth or other soft-soled shoes in order to feel stones and the roughness of the ground underfoot.

Just before Yom Kippur and the beginning of our 24-hour fast, we should eat a full meal (called seudah mafsket). To do so is a mitzvah. The meal following the fast should be light to accustom our stomachs to food again.

Appropriate colors for the table during the Days of Awe are white (purity) and blue (justice). On Yom Kippur eve use white only, or perhaps white and silver. But for the first meal after Yom Kippur, vibrant colors like yellow, green, gold, and orange express the catharsis of the Day of Atonement and our joyful confidence in the future.

The only required ceremonial objects for meals during the Days of Awe are the kiddush cup and candles. (If the holiday falls on a Friday night, add Sabbath candles and light the holiday candles first.)

ROSH HASHANAH: TRADITIONAL FOODS

Because of the widespread belief that what we eat on Rosh Hashanah influences our lives during the year, we abstain from eating sour, salty, bitter, and spicy foods. We place sugar in the saltcellar, and sprinkle the challah with sugar or dip it in honey. Some people do not drink coffee because of its color—black. Syrian Jews used to place a gold or silver coin in their wine cup to bring them wealth. In ancient times it was customary to put a sheep's head on the table as a token of our desire to be the head in life and not the tail—that is, to be successful. (The sheep is associated with the shofar and thus the ram sacrificed by Abraham when God stopped the sacrifice of Isaac.) Today, a fish head is eaten or at least placed on the table to express the wish for success.

Although no specific foods are obligatory on Rosh Hashanah, certain dishes have become traditional:

HONEY. We use honey as a dip and an ingredient in such recipes as honeycake and teglach to express our wish for a sweet year. Sugar or fruit juice may be used instead.

ROUND CHALLAH. The shape represents our hope for a year without problems, a smooth year. Other interpretations are that it symbolizes the crown of God's kingship or the cycle of the year. Sometimes the bread is shaped like a ladder or a bird, as a way of saying that we direct our prayers to heaven. We dip a piece of Challah in honey or sugar, unlike on the Sabbath, when it's customary to sprinkle salt on our bread.

APPLE. We begin our meal by dipping a slice of apple in honey, reciting the blessing "May it be Your will, O Lord our God, and God of our fathers, to renew unto us a happy and sweet year (Yehi ratzon mi'lfanecha Adonai Eloheynu ve'elohey avoteynu she'tehadesh aleynu shanah tovah u'metukah).

NEW FRUIT. On the second night we start the meal with a fruit we have not eaten during the year and recite the benediction shehehiyanu. Pious Jews deny themselves one fruit throughout the summer in order to have it that night.

CARROT.   Because carrots are sweet and lend themselves to preparation with honey or sugar in such dishes as kugel, they've become a standard component of Rosh Hashanah dinners.

POMEGRANATE.   Although not as traditional in the United States and Europe as the apple and other foods, the pomegranate is served by many families, particularly in Israel where it's abundant. It represents our resolve to become as full of wisdom as the fruit is full of seeds.

ROSH HASHANAH: MENUS

In addition to the dinners served on the first two nights of Rosh Hashanah, it's gracious to have a dessert table ready for people who drop in to wish us a Happy New Year.

DINNERS

Honey, sugar, or sweet fruit juice
Round challah
Apple slices
Fruit in addition to apples (second night)
Wine
Smoked white fish or gefilte fish (if meat is served), or
chopped chicken liver, or vegetable salad with honey-lime dressing
Chicken soup with rounds of carrots, or vegetable soup
Roast chicken in orange sauce, tsimmes stew, or baked stuffed fish
Carrot kugel
Sweet carrots
Pomegranate, with honey, apple, fruit, or carrot-pineapple
cake or teglach

DESSERT TABLE

Honey cake and/or fruitcake
Tea, coffee, soft drinks

ROSH HASHANAH: TABLE DECORATION

The Rosh Hashanah dinner and dessert tables should convey a soft and quiet feeling.

ROSH HASHANAH AND YOM KIPPUR

DINNERS

The traditional Rosh Hashanah dinner table consists of a white tablecloth with white napkins and candles, a family's best silverware, a vase of flowers for a centerpiece, and a slice of apple and some honey on a small plate at everyone's place setting. But the decoration can be enhanced without violating tradition.

On the first night, for example, place a bowl of fresh red apples with leaves in the center of the table between white candles. Surround the bowl with bright green leaves. Serve each person either an individual challah or a lady apple and a small cup or saucer of honey. Decorate the napkins with coins, and explain the Syrian custom of placing a coin in the wine glass. (Be sure to wash the coins first.) Ask guests to write their wishes for the coming year in a blank book or notebook representing the Book of Life.

For the children (and perhaps even if there aren't going to be any at the dinner), place figurines of small animals on the table. If anyone asks what they mean, tell the story about a rabbi who arrived late at Rosh Hashanah services because he had stopped on the way to feed the pets who had been neglected by the townspeople in their haste to get to the synagogue. The rabbi explained that God considers caring for the helpless to be more important than arriving at services on time.

Some alternative decorations include:

- Blue tablecloth with matching or white napkins.
- Centerpiece consisting of a row of candles (twelve or seven, representing the months or days of the week, or the number of people at the table). Or arrange the candles in a circle.
- Old-fashioned scale for a centerpiece, symbolizing justice.
- Figurine or toy sheep or ram and small altar made of sticks, as ornaments in addition to the centerpiece.
- Small New Year's greeting cards with guests' names, instead of ordinary place cards.

DESSERT TABLE

For convenience in serving guests who stop by during the holidays, use a sideboard or card table placed against the wall as a dessert table, and cover it with a white or blue tablecloth. Paper napkins are quite acceptable. Decorate the table by arranging greeting cards around a vase of flowers, preferably white if available. Or fasten greeting cards with scotch tape on the wall behind the table.

ROSH HASHANAH: CHECKLIST OF BASICS

Kiddush cup
Candles (at least two)
Wine
Honey
Apples

New fruit (second night)
Round Challah
Kipots (yarmulkes)

ROSH HASHANAH: MEMENTOS FOR GUESTS

Calendar for Jewish new year
Lady apples in miniature baskets
Miniature shofars
New Year's greeting cards
Small bottles of honey
Small calendars
Small notebooks

ROSH HASHANAH: GIFTS FOR THE HOST

Basket of fruit
Bottle of wine
Candy
Challah cover
Holiday dish
Honey dish
Honey or apple cake
Honey scoop
Jar of gourmet honey

SUMMARY OF SUGGESTED ORNAMENTS

Bowl of red apples
Coins
Candles
Flowers
Figurine of sheep or ram
Greeting cards with guests' names
Notebook
Scale (or weights)

YOM KIPPUR: TRADITIONAL FOODS

Dinner on Yom Kippur eve (before sundown on Tishri 9) should be a full meal—ample to sustain us for a day. Be sure to drink a lot of liquid to prevent dehydration during the fast: fruit juice, tea, or just water. The light meal we eat to break the fast should consist of dishes that can be prepared easily or in advance. As on Rosh Hashanah, certain foods are traditional but not required for the Yom Kippur eve dinner:

LADDER OR ROUND CHALLAH.   The ladder shape expresses the hope that our prayers will rise directly to heaven. If a ladder challah is not available, a round one expressing our wishes for a smooth year will do.

FISH.   It is believed that eating fish will bring fruitfulness and plenty during the year.

KREPLACH.   (Pockets of dough filled with chicken or meat.) The meat symbolizes God's judgment of us, and the dough represents the hope that His judgment will be wrapped in mercy.

YOM KIPPUR: MENUS

EVENING DINNER

The menu ordinarily is similar to what we serve Friday nights (see Sabbath, p. 8). But if the main course is chicken or meat, either gefilte fish or smoked fish would be the preferable appetizer. If the main course is fish (see, for example, the recipe for baked and stuffed fish), serve the chopped chicken liver as an appetizer. Put kreplach in the chicken soup, instead of noodles or rice.

LIGHT SUPPER

Ladder or round challah
Wine
Orange or other fruit juice
Vegetable soup (chicken-based)
Quiche, creamed eggs on toasted challah, or
lox and bagel with cream cheese
Green salad
Honey, apple, fruit cake
Hot or iced tea, coffee, or chocolate drink

or

Ladder or round challah
Wine
Orange or other fruit juice
Vegetable soup (chicken- or beef-based) or
chicken soup with kreplach
Sandwich steak on toast
Green salad
Fresh fruit salad or sorbet
Cookies
Hot or iced tea, coffee, or chocolate drink

ROSH HASHANAH AND YOM KIPPUR

YOM KIPPUR: TABLE DECORATION

DINNER

The same basic table setting used for Rosh Hashanah is appropriate for seudah mafseket, but the overall effect should be more frigid, more icy, in keeping with the solemnity of Yom Kippur. Use a white tablecloth with white napkins, white dishes, and silver or white candlesticks with white candles. For a traditional centerpiece, arrange white and purple or blue flowers in a clear glass, white, or silver vase. But you might introduce symbolism by replacing the flowers with a shofar and ram or sheep representing Abraham's sacrifice to God. Other decorations might include a Torah scroll and pointer.

LIGHT SUPPER

The mood for the meal breaking the fast, though, is optimistic and joyful. Use a colorful tablecloth — yellow, gold, green, or orange — with napkins of a different color. For the centerpiece, pile a bowl high with fresh fruit. Since many families begin to build the sukkah for the upcoming Sukkoth holiday after supper, place a hammer and nail next to the fruit bowl. In front of each place setting, put a little colored candle in a small glass. If your tablecloth is a solid color, place some mezuzahs and silver or gold paper stars on the table.

YOM KIPPUR: CHECKLIST

Fish (seudah mafseket)
Kiddush cup
Kreplach (seudah mafseket)
Ladder-shaped or round challah
White candles (seudah mafseket)
White linens (seudah mafseket)
Wine

RECIPES

GEFILTE FISH
(See Chapter 2, The Sabbath)

CHOPPED CHICKEN LIVER

Serves 6 or more

1 lb. fresh chicken livers
3 tbsp. chicken fat or 2 tbsp. vegetable oil
Salt to taste
Freshly ground black pepper to taste
1 hard-boiled egg (optional)
1-2 shallots or 1/2 medium-size onion, chopped
White radish, peeled and sliced (optional)

Wash chicken livers thoroughly in cold water. If chicken fat is used, melt it in skillet over medium heat. Add salt. Saute chopped shallots or onion in rendered fat or vegetable oil until translucent. Add chicken livers and saute until pink. Remove livers and shallots or onion, saving fat or oil. Be sure to retain crispy pieces of rendered fat. Chop livers, egg, by hand or in grinder, and mix in shallots or onion. *Do not puree. The texture should be coarse.* Add pepper generously and salt to taste. Gradually pour in fat, including crispy pieces, or oil until mixture is moist. Cover and refrigerate. Serve with matzo and, if desired, slices of radish.

VEGETABLE SALAD WITH HONEY-LIME DRESSING

Serves 4-6

2 raw carrots, sliced lengthwise
1 cold beet, sliced
1 cucumber, sliced
1 turnip, peeled and sliced
4-6 green onions (1 for each serving)
8-oz. can garbanzos (chickpeas)
1 head lettuce
1 large tomato, sliced, or a basket of cherry tomatoes
1/3-1/2 cup honey
Juice of 1 lime
Salt

Arrange chilled vegetables on bed of lettuce. Slowly stir lemon juice into honey, and add salt to taste. Pour dressing on salad just before serving.

CHICKEN SOUP
(See Chapter 2, Sabbath.)

VEGETABLE SOUP

Serves 6

3 carrots, diced
1 yellow onion, finely chopped
1/4 cup green pepper, chopped
2 medium size zucchini, sliced
3 stalks celery, sliced
1/4 cup green beans
1/4 cup Chinese sweet peas, cut into halves
1/4 cup green peas
2 large tomatoes, cut into small pieces
1/4 cup mushrooms, finely chopped
5 cups chicken broth
Salt and pepper to taste
3 tbsp. margarine

Saute carrots, onion, zucchini, pepper, and celery in margarine or vegetable oil until softened (about three minutes). Add hot chicken broth and simmer for 20 minutes. Add green beans, green peas, Chinese sweet peas, tomatoes, and mushrooms. Cook for additional 10 minutes. Add salt and pepper if desired. (Leftover diced meat or chicken may also be added.)

CHICKEN IN ORANGE SAUCE

Serves 4-6

One 3-4 lb. chicken, cut up
1 1/2 cups orange juice
1/2 cup toasted almonds, slivered
1/8 tsp. cinnamon
1/4 tsp. Tabasco
Pinch of ground cloves
1/2 cup raisins
1 orange, sectioned

Preheat oven to 375 degrees. Arrange chicken in oiled baking dish. Mix orange juice with almonds and spices and pour over chicken. Bake for 45 minutes. Add raisins and orange sections to juice at bottom of dish, baste chicken, and bake for additional 15 minutes. If desired, thicken sauce with flour, potato, or cornstarch.

TSIMMES STEW

Serves 4-6

2 lbs. beef brisket
8 carrots, sliced diagonally
3 yams, sliced
3 large white potatoes, sliced
4 tbsp. oil
1/2 cup honey
1/8 tsp. salt
1/8 tsp. black pepper
Water, as needed

Heat oil in large, deep pot, and brown brisket on all sides. Place carrots, yams, and potatoes around the meat and add salt, pepper, and honey. Cover with water, bring to boil, then lower heat and cook for two hours. Slice meat, surround with vegetables, and serve.

BAKED STUFFED FISH

Serves 6-8

1 large or medium whole fish (bass, flounder, halibut—
*   any fresh or saltwater fish)*
4 cups bread cubes, stale or toasted
1/2 cup chicken stock
1 whole shallot or small onion, diced
1/2 cup celery, minced or diced
2 baby carrots or 1 medium carrot, diced
1 medium bell pepper (green, red, or yellow), diced
1 clove garlic, minced (or 1/2 tsp. garlic powder)
1/2 cube margarine
1/2 tsp. thyme
Dash of sage
1 tsp. lemon grass (optional)
1 tsp. salt
Pepper to taste
1 lemon or lime, sliced
Parsley

Preheat oven to 350 degrees. Saute celery, carrots, bell bepper, garlic, and shallot in margarine until wilted and translucent, but not brown. Add seasonings and stir well. Put bread cubes in bowl, add sauted vegetables, pour heated chicken stock over everything, and toss. Rinse fish in cold water, rub with lemon, and salt lightly (inside and out). Pack stuffing into fish and rub outside lightly with vegetable oil or margarine. Bake for 15 minutes, then test by gently inserting a fork and lifting a tiny piece of the fish. If it flakes easily, it is done. Do not overcook. (Usually takes about 1/2 hour, depending on the thickness of the fish.) Serve on an oblong platter, surrounded by parsley and lemon or lime wedges.

CARROT KUGEL

Serves 4-6

1 cup margarine
2 cups brown sugar
2 egg yolks
1 cup carrots, grated
1 tbsp. water
1 tsp. vanilla
1 1/4 cups flour
2 tsp. baking powder
2 egg whites

Preheat oven to 350 degrees. Cream together margarine, brown sugar, egg yolks, carrots, water, and vanilla, then mix with flour and baking powder. Beat egg whites until they form stiff peaks, then fold into the batter. Pour into greased 10-inch round spring-form pan or 9x13-inch pan and bake for one hour.

SWEET CARROTS

Serves 4

6 carrots, cut into 1/4-inch rounds
1/2 cup prunes, pitted
1/2 cup orange juice
1 cinnamon stick

Place sliced carrots in pot, add prunes (to taste) and cinnamon stick. Cover with orange juice and bring to boil. Reduce heat amd simmer for a very long time, either on top of stove or in oven. Serve hot, when sauce has thickened.

HONEY CAKE

Serves 6-8

1 1/4 cups honey
1 cup oil
2 tsp. instant coffee, mixed with 1/2 cup boiling water
1 1/4 cup brown sugar
4 eggs
4 cups self-rising flour
1 tsp. baking soda
1/2 tsp. cinnamon

Preheat oven to 325 degrees. Mix honey, oil, coffee, and sugar until smooth. Add eggs, mix thoroughly, then slowly add flour, baking soda, and cinnamon. Stir until smooth and place in 12x10x3-inch pan greased with margarine or oil. Bake for 1 to 1 1/4 hours.

GRATED APPLE CAKE

Serves 6-8

2 eggs
1 cup sugar
1 cup powdered sugar
1 cup oil
1 tsp. vanilla
1 tsp. salt
2 tsp. baking soda
1 tsp. cinnamon
2 cups flour
4 green apples, grated
1 cup walnuts, chopped

Preheat oven to 350 degrees. Cream eggs with sugar in mixer until smooth. Add oil and vanilla and mix well. Sift flour with salt, baking soda, and cinnamon and add to mixture, then fold in apples and nuts. Pour into greased 10-inch round pan and bake for 55-60 minutes, then sprinkle with powdered sugar.

FRUITCAKE

Serves 6-8

2 pkgs. coconut cookies, crumbled
Four or five 8-oz. cans fruit, drained. Use pineapple,
*   apricot, peach, or pear.*
1 tsp. sherry
1 tsp. fruit juice

Preheat oven to 350 degrees. Grease 13x9-inch Pyrex dish with margarine and cover bottom with one package of crumbled cookies. Arrange fruit in layers on top of the cookie crumbs. Cover with the other package of cookies and wet the crumbs with sherry and fruit juice. Bake 45-60 minutes.

TEGLACH

Serves 20

2 lbs. honey
1 lb. brown sugar
8 eggs
1/2 cup salad oil
About 4 1/2 cups flour
1 tsp. baking powder
Granulated sugar
Pinch of cinnamon or ginger

Mix honey and brown sugar in large pot and slowly bring to boil. Cook until mixture starts to darken and thicken slightly. Beat eggs together with oil; add flour and baking powder and mix until dough is easy to handle. Roll walnut-size pieces of dough between palms to form ropes. Tie into knots, tuck in ends to form knotted balls, and drop into the boiling honey and brown sugar mixture. Cook until they reach a nice brown color. To test, remove a ball from the pot and drop it into cold water. If done, a crust will form. When the last ball is removed from the honey, immediately add one cup strong tea or coffee, remove from heat, and stir well. (Set aside and use to make honey cake.) Roll the teglach in granulated sugar mixed with a pinch of cinnamon or ginger. Option: before cooking, tie a raisin or two into each knot.

CARROT-PINEAPPLE CAKE

Serves 6-8

1 cup margarine
2 cups sugar
3 eggs
2 1/2 cups flour
1/2 tsp. salt
1 1/2 tsp. cinnamon
2 tsp. baking soda
2 tsp. vanilla
1 cup carrots, grated
1 cup crushed pineapple, drained
1 cup unsweetened coconut, grated
1 cup walnuts, chopped

Preheat oven to 325 degrees. Mix margarine and sugar, then add beaten eggs and stir. Sift flour with salt, cinnamon, and baking soda and slowly add to mixture. When smooth, add remaining ingredients and pour into greased 10-inch round pan. Bake for 1 1/4 hours.

KREPLACH

Serves 4

Dough
1 egg
1 cup flour, sifted
1/2 tsp. salt
2 tbsp. oil

Mix ingredients thoroughly, knead, and roll into thin sheet. Cut into two-inch squares.

Filling
1/4 lb. ground meat
3 tbsp. onion, minced
2 tbsp. walnuts, minced
1/8 tsp. paprika
Salt and pepper to taste

Mix ingredients and place one tsp. on each square of dough. Fold into triangles, pinch the open sides together, drop into boiling water, and cook for 20 minutes. To serve, heat chicken soup and add kreplach. Option: Cook in boiling chicken soup.

CREAMED EGGS ON TOAST

Serves 2-3

6 eggs
1 cup milk
1 tsp. parsley, minced (save sprigs)
2 tbsp. butter
2 tbsp. flour
Salt and pepper to taste
2 tbsp. heavy cream
4-6 pieces of toast
Optional:
    Dash of nutmeg
    Thin slice of onion or onion powder

Boil eggs slowly until hard (about 10 minutes). Meanwhile, mix milk with onion and parsley, and bring just to the boiling point (but do not allow to boil). Melt butter in separate pan and stir in flour, a little at a time so it doesn't lump. (Use a wire whisk, if available.) Pour hot milk into flour and butter mixture very slowly, stirring vigorously. Simmer gently for about five minutes, stirring occasionally. If the sauce gets too thick, stir in a little more milk. Add salt, pepper, and cream. Stir, then remove from heat.

Shell and slice the eggs crosswise into even pieces. Toast bread, and place egg slices on toast in a nice overlapping pattern. (To serve without toast, place egg slices on plate.) Pour the sauce over the eggs, covering completely. Garnish with parsley sprigs and serve while hot. (Recipe makes about 1 1/2 cups sauce.)

Less-Rich Sauce
2 tbsp. butter
2 tbsp. flour
1 cup milk
Salt and pepper to taste
Dash of nutmeg or other herbal seasoning (optional)

Melt butter in saucepan. Do not allow to brown. Slowly add flour, whisking or beating it into the butter. Heat milk to boiling point in separate pan and add to butter and flour, stirring mixture while pouring. Heat mixture until it comes to a boil and thickens. If necessary, simmer slowly to produce creamy consistency. Add salt and pepper, and pour over eggs.

CREAMED EGGS ON TOAST
(Easy Way)

1 can cream of mushroom or cream of celery soup
1 cup milk
1 tsp. butter
2 tbsp. flour
Salt and pepper to taste

Mix soup and milk and bring to a boil, add butter, and stir. Slowly add flour, sprinkling it into the simmering mixture so it doesn't lump. Simmer four to five minutes. Add salt and pepper to taste and pour over sliced boiled eggs. If mixture is too thin, add a little more flour and simmer until it is absorbed. (Flour must be cooked so it doesn't taste raw.)

CHAPTER 4

Sukkoth
(Tishri 15–21: Late September or Early October)
and
Simhath Torah
(Tishri 23: Late September or Early October)

On the fifteenth day of the seventh month, when you have gathered in the fruits of the land, you shall keep the fruits of the land, you shall keep the feast of the Lord seven days; on the first day shall be a solemn rest, and on the eighth day shall be a solemn rest. And you shall take you on the first day the fruit of goodly trees, branches of palm trees, and boughs of thick trees, and willows of the brook, and you shall rejoice before the Lord your God seven days. . . . You shall dwell in booths seven days; all that are homeborn in Israel shall dwell in booths; that your generations may know that I made the children of Israel to dwell in booths, when I brought them out of the land of Egypt.

Leviticus 23: 39-43

For entertaining, Sukkoth is the ultimate holiday. Generosity and sharing are a basic part of the celebration, because Sukkoth is a festival of thanksgiving for the harvest. Hence it is also known as Hag Ha-sif, the feast of ingathering.

The name Sukkoth, however, is the plural of the word sukkah meaning hut or booth, and refers to the shelters in which the Israelites lived for forty years while wandering in the desert after the exodus from Egypt. During the week-long festival we are enjoined by the Torah to live in huts outside our homes. But the ever-practical Talmudic rabbis ruled that it's all right just to have meals in the sukkah, and if that's uncomfortable due to inclement weather or cramped quarters it's sufficient to say kiddush and break bread there. Part of the fun of the holiday is the tradition of visiting relatives' and friends' sukkahs for the kiddush. With a little scheduling, the visits could be turned into a round of parties, even if only wine and dessert are served. It is a mitzvah to invite the homeless and other people who do not have a sukkah, especially on the first night. A charming custom introduced by the Cabalists is to set aside a chair at the table for visits by our biblical forefathers. In some households invitations are written to these ushpizim, or spiritual guests, and placed on the table in front of their chair.

The Talmud is quite specific about how to construct a sukkah. It must have at least three sides, which can be built from any material. Today, most families use canvas or plywood attached to a wooden or metal frame. But the roof must be made of something that grows in the soil—branches, thatch, or bamboo—and should be loosely constructed so that the sky is visible through the material. The sukkah may be any size, but at least large enough to accommodate one person and a table. Since it's a mitzvah to beautify this temporary home, many people decorate it with tapestries, pictures (the Holy Land is a favorite subject), charms, or fruits and vegetables, especially those mentioned in the Bible. Traditionally, construction of the sukkah begins right after Yom Kippur, marking the transition from the solemn Days of Awe to Zeman Simhatenu, the time of our rejoicing, as Sukkoth is sometimes called.

On the seventh day of Sukkoth, the mood suddenly changes again. Named Hoshanah Rabbah, meaning save us or help us, it is similar in some respects to the High Holidays. The theme is penitence and rebirth. Tradition has it that until Hoshanah Rabbah the judgments entered in the Book of Life on Rosh Hashanah can be changed. It is also believed by some that if you see your shadow on the eve of the holiday you can tell whether you are destined to live or die during the year. If the shadow has no head, your death is ordained. Another belief is that at midnight on Hoshanah Rabbah the skies open and wishes made to heaven come true. Yet with the underlying solemnity there is a spirit of exultation as worshippers in the synagogue beat willow branches on the floor until the leaves fall off, symbolically casting off sin. (Another interpretation is that the falling leaves represent rain drops and thus rebirth of the land following the dry summer in the Holy Land.) After services it is customary to return home for a joyful last meal of the festival.

Two independent holidays, Shemini Atzereth and Simhath Torah, have been appended to Sukkoth over the years and are generally considered eighth and ninth days of the festival. In Israel they are both celebrated on the eighth day.

Shemini Atzereth is devoted primarily to supplications for rain, and thereafter a prayer for rain is said daily until Passover. At the time of the Second Temple the altar was decorated every day with fresh willow branches, symbols for water. Even now many of the Orthodox in Jerusalem buy fresh willow from someone in the synagogue every day between Shemini Atzereth and Passover.

While the Torah orders us to observe Shemini Atzereth as a "day of solemn assembly," Simhath Torah is not mentioned anywhere in the Bible or the Talmud. Originally, it was the "second day of the Diaspora" for Shemini Atzereth, but around the tenth century it was given its present name, which means rejoicing in the Torah. It marks the end of the annual cycle of reading the Torah and the start of a new cycle.

Simhath Torah is the most joyful of all the holidays. In the synagogue the congregation sings and dances while the Torah is carried around the reading platform (bimah) seven times. For children it is an especially exciting celebration. They're encouraged to join boisterously in the singing and dancing as they wave Simhath Torah flags and miniature Torahs they've been given to make the celebration even more fun. After three adults in the congregation have read from the Torah—a special honor—the children are invited up to the bimah to pronounce a blessing over the Torah, a privilege reserved on all other days for only those who are Bar Mitzvah.

SUKKOTH

CEREMONIAL OBJECTS

In accordance with a command in Leviticus, four growing things called arba hamminim in Hebrew are placed in the sukkah during the seven days of the festival: citron (ethrog), a palm branch (alulav), myrtle (hadas), and willow (arava). Because of their ritualistic importance, they must be of excellent quality. The citron has to be yellow like a ripe lemon and without spots. Its nipple (pitom) must be intact, and therefore the box for the citron should be lined with soft material for protection. The foliage on the other hamminim must be green. Every morning we place citron in a special box and tie the palm branch, myrtle, and willow together, and as we recite a blessing shake them in all directions to indicate that God surrounds us.

Various meanings have been ascribed to the hamminim. One interpretation is that they represent human physiology. Citron stands for the heart, the palm branch for the spine, myrtle for the eyes, and willow for mouth. Another is that they symbolize four different types of Jew. Since the citron tastes good and has aroma, it represents Jews who do good deeds and are knowledgeable about the Torah. The fruit of the palm tastes good but has no aroma, and therefore stands for people who do good deeds but do not know the Torah. Because myrtle is tasteless but smells good, it symbolizes people who do not do good deeds but are educated. Willow, which has neither flavor not fragrance, stands for those do not do good deeds and are ignorant. Together the four types comprise the Jewish people as a whole.

As on other holidays mentioned in the Torah, two candles must be placed on the dining table the first night of Sukkoth. But unlike on the Sabbath, the blessing is said before the candles are lit. If the first night falls on the Sabbath, we light the festival candles, then recite the blessing and light the Sabbath candles.

MENU

No particular dish is associated with Sukkoth, but it is traditional to eat a vegetable stuffed with ground meat. Because the holiday is a harvest celebration, the menu should emphasize vegetables. A typical menu would be:

> *Fruit juice, or half a grapefruit*
> *Vegetable soup*
> *Green or red bell peppers, cabbage, grape leaves,*
> *acorn squash, or zucchini stuffed with ground meat*
> *Mashed white potatoes or baked yams*
> *Mixed green salad*
> *Parve chocolate-orange cake*

TABLE DECORATION

Harvest colors like brown, orange, yellow, dark green, and gold are appropriate for Sukkoth table decorations. To add to the excitement of the festival, you might want to change the style of the decoration every day – and do something really different on Hoshanah Rabbah and Shemini Atzeeret.

As your basic setting, use a brown tablecloth and for color fold brown napkins around orange or green ones. Insert a few stalks of wheat in napkin rings made of straw or ribbons. For a centerpiece, group fruit around the citron container and garnish with leaves to suggest trees. To enhance the decoration, add a figurine of a camel or a miniature tent (representing the desert) or a figurine of a farmer. Place stalks of wheat around the table.

Slight variations in the decoration can change the look of the table and thus the feeling inside the sukkah:

LINENS. You can express the joyfulness of the holiday by using colorful table coverings, especially if you combine colors. For example –

- Place mats on the tablecloth and/or alternate brown, tan, green, orange, yellow, gold, or floral tablecloths and matching or contrasting napkins.

- Use the same tablecloth all the time, but create a two-tone diamond-like effect by putting another of a different color on top of it with the corners facing the ends of the table. In addition to the traditional fall color combination of brown with orange or yellow, some interesting combinations are a rich brown or green with gold (which symbolizes prosperity), cream, or a floral pattern; stark white on dark brown; cocoa brown and cream or light green (but not a very bright green).

- If you have an oriental throw rug, it would be an elegant and unusual touch to use it as a tablecloth or base for the centerpiece as a reminder of the traditional flooring for tents.

CENTERPIECES. By changing the centerpiece, you can represent different aspects of the Sukkoth story. For example –

- On a runner along the center of the table, place symbols of the holiday, such as miniature chairs for the ushpizim, small baskets of fruit, a miniature Torah, wheat, vegetables, miniature farm tools, figurines of farmers, and miniature musical instruments (reminiscent of the joyful processions of pilgrims who converged on Jerusalem to celebrate the holiday). You might start out with just a few elements, then add more every day.

- Arrange small gardening tools, such as trowels and shears, on a bed of leaves and form a border around them with carrots, green onions, tomatoes, zucchini, cucumbers.

- On a map of Israel, place a miniature tent or a sukkah with figurines of farmers and stalks of wheat.

- Fill a low wicker basket with vegetables.

HOSHANAH RABBAH. Use a white or gray tablecloth, with blue napkins, and down the center of the table place a wide blue runner or wide blue ribbons. (The white or gray symbolizes clouds, and the blue the sky.) Invite your family and guests to write their wishes for the year in chalk on the runner or ribbons. Put the candles at the ends of the table and surround them with flowers.

SHEMINI ATZERET. Retaining the same white or gray tablecloth and blue napkins used for Hoshanah Rabbah, scatter blue dots (representing water) around the table and tie gray ribbons around the napkins. (Or use white or gray napkins and tie blue ribbons around them.) Down the middle of the table arrange some willow branches and in the center put a pitcher of water between two colorful candles as an expression of optimism. On one side of the water pitcher build a miniature altar out of wooden matches or toothpicks, recalling the practice of pouring water on the altar of the Temple in Jerusalem during prayers for rain.

GIFTS FOR THE HOST

Basket of fruit
Book about Sukkoth
Citron container
Fruit cake
Picture of Israel, charm, or other decoration for the sukkah
Wine

MEMENTOS FOR GUESTS

Bookmarks decorated with pictures of the Holy Land
Bouquets of multi-colored wheat stalks
Citrons
Small straw baskets filled with tiny vegetables and fruit like cocktail
    corn, cherry tomatoes, cocktail onions, olives, grapes

CHECKLIST OF CEREMONIAL OBJECTS

Citron
Palm branch
Myrtle
Willow
Kiddush cup
Wine
Candles
Kipots (yarmulkes)

SUMMARY OF SUGGESTED ORNAMENTS

Altar (miniature, made of matches or toothpicks)
Artificial fruit
Chairs (miniature)
Farm tools (miniature)
Figurine of camel
Figurines of farmers
Fruit baskets (small)
Gardening tools
Oriental rug
Sukkah (miniature)
Tent (miniature)
Vegetables
Water pitcher (Shemini Atzeret)
Wheat stalks
Wicker basket filled with vegetables
Willow branches (Shemini Atzeret)

SIMHATH TORAH

No special ceremonial objects are required for Simhath Torah, except the kiddush cup, wine, and candles, of course. Nor are any particular foods traditional. Dishes served during the Sukkoth festival are appropriate, particularly meat-stuffed ones, but by this time the family might like a bit of a change.

MENU

> *Fried dates or prunes stuffed with meat (appetizer)*
> *Chicken soup*
> *Chicken in orange sauce*
> *Steamed rice*
> *Chopped eggplant, or carrot salad, or lettuce-orange salad*
> *Peach or apricot halves filled with cranberry sauce*
> *Walnut cookies*

TABLE DECORATION

Because it celebrates the Torah, the holiday is best represented by royal colors—purple, blue, deep green, or gold. If you have linens in one of these colors, use them. Otherwise use white and place a smaller royal-colored paper tablecloth diagonally across it, with the corners draped over the sides of the table. The candles should be white. (Instead of using regular candle holders, you might core green apples and place candles in the holes. The candles should be fairly short, otherwise they'll tip over.) In the center of the table place a cardboard tree—or a real one, if you're fortunate enough to have a bonsai. On the branches hang ten Simhath Torah flags or small cards cut into the shape of the Tablets of the Law, and on each write one of the commandments. Put a miniature Torah next to the tree, and surround it with maple sugar or candy because the Torah is sweet. Scatter unpopped corn around the table, symbolizing the manna God provided the Israelites during their wanderings in the dessert.

GIFTS FOR THE HOST

Bonsai tree
Box of candy
Cake, especially a very sweet one
Candle holders
Flowers
Miniature Torah
Picture frame in shape of Torah or tablets of the law
Rimonim (Torah decorations)

MEMENTOS FOR GUESTS

Artificial miniature trees (because the Torah is the tree of life)
Crowns made of candy or paper (because the Torah is king)
Napkin rings made out of strips of colored paper pasted at the
    ends, inscribed with quotations from the Torah
Simhath Torah flags
Torah scrolls (miniature)

RECIPES

VEGETABLE SOUP

3 carrots, diced   Serves 6
1 yellow onion, finely diced
1/4 cup green pepper, chopped
2 medium size zucchini, sliced
3 stalks celery, sliced
1/4 cup green beans, cut in pieces
1/4 cup Chinese sweet peas, cut into halves
1/4 cup green peas
2 large tomatoes, cut into small pieces
1/4 cup mushrooms, finely chopped
5 cups chicken broth
Salt and pepper to taste
3 tbsp. margarine

Saute carrots, onion, zucchini, pepper, and celery in margarine or vegetable oil until softened (about three minutes). Add hot chicken broth and simmer for 20 minutes. Add green beans, green peas, Chinese sweet peas, tomatoes, and mushrooms. Cook for additional 10 minutes. Add salt and pepper if desired. (Leftover diced meat or chicken may also be added.)

STUFFED GRAPE LEAVES, CABBAGE, GREEN OR RED PEPPERS, ACORN SQUASH, OR ZUCCHINI

Stuffing   Serves 6
1 lb. ground beef
2 large garlic cloves, chopped fine
2 large onions, chopped fine
1/2 cup rice, soy granules, or matzo meal
Salt and pepper to taste

Sprinkle salt and pepper onto meat. Fry onions and garlic until yellow and soft. Add rice, soy granules, or matzo meal, and fry a little longer, then thoroughly mix with meat. For stuffed grape leaves, add mint and pine nuts. Preheat oven to 350 degrees.

Grape Leaves   Serves 8-12
3 doz. grape leaves
1/2 cup white wine
Mint, to taste

Put grape leaves in a bowl, pour boiling water over them, and let stand for five minutes or until soft. Place one tsp. stuffing on each leaf and roll into a packet with ends tucked in. Pack into casserole, pour white wine over them, add enough water to cover, stew a little mint across the top, and bake for about 1/2 hour. Add water or wine if needed.

Cabbage Leaves

Serves 8-12

12 large cabbage leaves
Two 6-oz. cans tomato paste
1/4 cup lemon juice
1/4 cup mild Mexican salsa (jar or can)

Soften cabbage leaves in very hot water for five minutes, or blanch in boiling water for one or two minutes. Do not overcook. Put enough stuffing on each leaf to form a large packet when rolled up. Tuck in ends as snugly as possible. Place in casserole. Pour on tomato paste, mixed with lemon juice and salsa. Bake for about 1 1/2 hours.

Peppers

Serves 6

6 green or red peppers
2-oz. can tomato paste
1/4 cup lemon juice
1/4 cup mild Mexican salsa (jar or can)
Mint or pine nuts to taste

Remove tops and seeds from peppers, parboil, and allow to cool. Fill with stuffing, adding mint or pine nuts if desired, and place in casserole. Mix tomato paste with 1/4 cup lemon juice and 1/4 cup mild salsa and pour over peppers. Bake for about one hour.

Acorn Squash

Serves 12

3 acorn squash
1/4 cup lemon juice
1/4 lb. or less margarine

Cut squash in half lengthwise. Clean out seeds and strings, rub the cut surfaces with margarine, fill center with lemon juice, place cut side down in pan, and bake until soft. Allow to cool, scoop out flesh, mix with stuffing, and refill shells. Bake for about 1/2 hour. Each half serves two.

Zucchini

Serves 6-8

2 lbs. small to medium zucchini
1/4 cup lemon juice
1/4 lb. margarine

Scrub zucchini and cut off tip ends. Boil for about five minutes. Allow to cool, and cut in half lengthwise. Scoop out flesh, chop, add to stuffing, and refill shells. Sprinkle with margarine. Bake for about 1/2 hour.

MASHED WHITE POTATOES AND YAMS

Serves 6

1 lb. long white potatoes
1 lb. yams
1/3 cup chicken broth
1/4 cup margarine (optional)
Salt and pepper to taste

Peel potatoes, cut into pieces, and immediately cover with cold water in three-quart pan. Boil until soft (20-30 minutes). Drain, mash, add chicken broth or margarine, and beat until blended. Season with salt and pepper. Use ice cream scoop to serve. (Alternative: To preserve nutrients, do not peel potatoes until they are cooked. When water comes to boil, cover pan and reduce heat to medium. When tender, hold under cold water, slip off skins, and follow instructions above.)

CHOCOLATE-ORANGE CAKE

Serves 10

2 cups flour
1 1/2 cups sugar
6 eggs
1/2 cup oil
3/4 cup orange juice
4 oz. chocolate chips, unsweetened
1 cup walnuts, chopped
2 tsp. baking powder

Separate eggs and beat whites until stiff. Preheat oven to 350 degrees. Mix sugar, oil, and egg yolks until smooth. Add juice, chocolate, and walnuts. Slowly add flour and baking powder while mixing. When well mixed, carefully fold in egg whites. Pour into 10-cup muffin tin. (Grease the cups lightly with margarine or vegetable oil to prevent sticking.) Bake for 25-35 minutes.

DATES OR PRUNES STUFFED WITH MEAT

(Serve as first course or as hors d'oeuvre.)   Serves 10 or more

45 dates
1/4 lb. ground meat
1 egg yolk
1/4 cup diced walnuts
Salt and pepper to taste
Olive oil
Juice of 1 lemon

Pit the dates. Mix meat with egg yolk, walnuts, salt, and pepper and stuff into dates. Coat the bottom of a deep frying pan with olive oil and simmer the dates until they expand. Cover with water, add lemon juice, and cook over low heat for about one hour.

CHICKEN IN ORANGE SAUCE

Serves 4-6

3 lbs. chicken parts
3 tbsp. oil
1/2 cup white wine
3 tbsp. catsup
1/2 cup chicken broth (or chicken bouillon cubes,
dissolved in boiling water)
2 oranges, sliced
1 lemon, sliced
1/2 cup orange juice
1 tbsp. cornstarch, mixed with 3 tbsp. water
1 tsp. sugar

Saute chicken quickly in the oil, then place in large pot. Add wine, catsup, and broth. Bring to boil, then simmer for 15 minutes. Add orange and lemon slices, orange juice, sugar, and cornstarch, then cook for another five to ten minutes. Before serving, decorate with fresh orange slices.

CHOPPED EGGPLANT

Serves 6

1 eggplant (about 1 lb.)
1/3 cup salad oil, or a little less
1 large or 2 medium onions
3 cloves (or more) garlic
One 6-oz. can tomato paste
1-2 tbsp. lemon juice
Optional:
1/4 cup medium salsa
1 tsp. salt
1/8 tsp. pepper

Wash eggplant thoroughly, cut off top and bottom, but do not peel. Dice into 1/2-inch cubes. Place in hot oil in 10-inch heavy skillet and cook over moderate heat, stirring frequently, until fairly soft (about 10-15 minutes). Chop onions coarsely and mince garlic, remove eggplant from skillet with slotted spoon, and cook onions and garlic until golden and soft. Put eggplant back in the pan, add the rest of the ingredients, stir well, cover, and simmer. The sauce will thicken in 35-45 minutes, and the eggplant will be very tender. Serve warm or cold, as a dinner vegetable or as an appetizer with crackers.

CARROT SALAD

Serves 6-8

2 lbs. carrots, peeled and shredded
1/4-1/2 cup almonds, chopped
1 can mandarin oranges, drained
Juice of 4-6 oranges
Juice of 1 lemon
1/4 cup raisins
6 dates, chopped

Mix orange and lemon juice with carrots, almonds, raisins, dates, and mandarin oranges in large bowl. Place in refrigerator for a few hours. To serve, fill skin of 1/2 orange with salad and place on doily on small plate.

LETTUCE-ORANGE SALAD

Serves 6

1 romaine lettuce
1 butter lettuce
3 oranges or can of mandarin oranges, drained
1/2 cup black olives, chopped
1/2 cup walnuts, chopped
1/4 cup olive oil
1/4 cup lemon juice
2 cloves garlic, minced
1/4 tsp. salt
1/8 tsp. white pepper

Wash lettuce and dry. Cut or tear into bite-size pieces. Peel and slice oranges. Place olive oil, lemon juice, garlic, white pepper, and salt in a jar and shake well. Place a layer of lettuce in a large bowl and cover it with a layer of oranges, then spread a little dressing on top. Repeat. Use the rest of the lettuce and oranges to make additional layers. Decorate with olives and walnuts.

WALNUT COOKIES

Serves 6

2 cups walnuts, chopped fine
1/2 cup margarine
1/2 cup oil
1/2 cup sugar
2 tsp. vanilla
2 cups flour
1/2 tsp. baking soda

Preheat oven to 325 degrees. Blend margarine, oil, sugar, and vanilla in mixer until smooth. Add walnuts, flour, and baking soda, and mix well by hand. Shape into balls the size of walnuts, place about one inch apart on ungreased baking sheet, and bake 15-20 minutes.

CHAPTER 5

Hanukkah
(Kislev 25–Tevet 3: December)

King Antiochus . . . sent letters to Jerusalem and the cities of Judah that they should profane the Sabbaths and feasts, pollute the sanctuary, and build altars and temples and shrines for idols . . . And in those days rose up Mattathias, a priest from Jerusalem . . . And Mattathias cried out...with a loud voice saying, "Whosoever is for the Law, and maintains the Covenant, let him follow me. . . . " The days of Mattathias drew near that he should die, and his son Judah [Maccabeus] rose up in his stead. . . . King Antiochus sent forty thousand foot soldiers and seven thousand horses, to go into the land of Judea. . . . And they that were with Judah joined battle, and the heathens were discomfited when they saw the boldness of them who were with Judah, and how they were ready either to live or die nobly. And Judah and his brethren said, "Behold our enemies are discomfited, let us go up to cleanse the Sanctuary, and to dedicate it afresh."

I Maccabees 1:41–4:37

The revolt of the Maccabees, which we commemorate on Hanukkah, is one of the most glorious episodes in the ongoing struggle of the Jewish people to preserve our unique heritage. As the renowned scholar Rabbi J. H. Hertz said, "There is nothing finer in the whole history of heroism, or more soul-stirring in the annals of religion, than the account of this handful of Jewish warriors who were prepared to live or die nobly in order that the light of revealed truth and righteousness be not extinguished in a heathen world."[1] The story of the revolt is told in two Apocryphal books that are sometimes attached to the Bible, I and II Maccabees.

In 167 B.C.E. the Seleucid King Antiochus IV issued a decree forbidding the Jews to observe the Sabbath and practice circumcision, and he rededicated the Jerusalem Temple to the Greek god Zeus. Ruler of Mesopotamia and Syria, including the Holy Land, Antiochus was determined to impose Greek institutions throughout his vast kingdom as a means of unifying it. Some wealthy Jews had already adopted aspects of Greek culture. The first book of Maccabees relates that "they built a gymnasium in Jerusalem, such as the pagans have, disguised their circumcision, and abandoned the holy covenant, submitting to the heathen rule as willing slaves of impiety."[2]

When king's officers attempted to force the Judean village of Modein to sacrifice an

---

[1] J. H. Hertz, *The Pentateuch and Haftorahs* (London: Soncino Press, 1964), p. 991.

[2] I Maccabees 1:15–16.

animal (possibly a pig) to a Greek god, an elderly priest named Mattathias refused. He killed a Jew who was about to comply and the officer who had given the order. Mattathias then fled with his five sons to the Gophna hills, where they were joined by the Hasidim and a number of other Jews, mostly common people. Led by the old priest, the exiles launched a guerrilla war against the king's forces.

Mattathias died in 166 and was succeeded by his son Judah, known to history as Judah Maccabee or Judas Maccabaeus. Judah repeatedly attacked the Seleucid army until in 164 he captured Jerusalem. On Kislev 25 the Temple was reconsecrated "to the sound of zithers, harps, and cymbals," and the celebration lasted eight days. Judah and the assembly then decreed that henceforth the anniversary of the reconsecration should be celebrated for eight days every year. Hanukkah means dedication. It was the first Jewish holiday not based on the Torah.

In addition to commemorating the victory of the Maccabees, we celebrate a miracle that is said to have occurred when the Temple was rededicated. After cleaning out the Temple, Judah's companions searched for sacramental oil to reignite the Eternal Light, but all they could find was barely enough for one day. Nevertheless, the light burned steadily until a supply of oil was delivered eight days later. We recall the miracle by lighting the eight candles of the special Hanukkah menorah called the hanukiah. Hence the holiday is also known as the Festival of Lights.

Because Hanukkah is not a Torah holiday, the celebration is flexible and easy-going. It can be a lot of fun, especially for children. Since the Middle Ages it has been customary to clear the table after a sumptuous dinner and play games. Then, as now, card games were popular, despite efforts by the rabbis to discourage them. Charades and puzzles were also favorite pastimes, and still are in some families.

But the traditional Hanukkah game is dreidel, or Put and Take. According to Jewish lore, dreidel originated among Jewish students when Antiochus IV outlawed the Torah (he actually never went quite that far). If the king's soldiers appeared while the students were studying the Torah, they would hide the sacred scrolls and pretend to be gambling with a dreidel, a Yiddish word meaning "something that spins." The dreidel is a top with four sides, on each of which a Hebrew letter is inscribed: nun, gimel, he, or shin, which are the initials of the Hebrew words *nes gadol haya sham,* "a great miracle happened there" and of the Yiddish words *nem* (take) or *nisht* (nothing), *gib* (give) or *gentz* (all), *halb* (half), and *shtel* (put). In Israel the letter pe, standing for the word *po* which means "here" is substituted for shin, because the miracle occurred in the Holy Land.

At the beginning of each game of dreidel, the players put a specified amount of money or chips or whatever in the pot. Then proceeding one at a time around the table, they spin the top. If the letter nun is upward when the spinning stops, the player passes. If it's gimel, the player wins the entire pot—and the game starts over. The letter he awards the winner half the pot. The letter shin obliges the player to put another coin in the pot.

For children the most fun is probably the custom of giving them money. In the United States the tradition has evolved into gift giving, not only to children but also among adults. This resulted from the pressures on families of the American commercialization of Christmas, which falls about the same time as Hanukkah.

Happiness and congeniality best describe the mood of the holiday. Appropriate colors are blue for justice, white for truth, gold for Jerusalem (it was also the color of the lamp for the Eternal Light), and red for the blood lost by the followers of the Maccabees.

THE HANUKIAH

The only ceremonial object required for Hanukkah is the special menorah (candelabrum), the hanukiah. Because the holiday is not mentioned in the Torah, we do not say kiddush before dinner (except on Friday night, of course). And we light the candles after sundown, not before, so that the flames will be visible from outside the house. (They may be kindled any time up to midnight, to allow time for the entire family to get home from work.) Before the rise of violent anti-Semitism, the ceremony was performed at the front door, opposite the mezuzah. But when it became dangerous to be identified as a Jew, the ceremony was moved inside. We now place the hanukiah on a window sill, although it may be put anywhere the family gathers.

Around the time of the destruction of the Second Temple, there was a debate among the followers of the great rabbis Shammai and Hillel about how the Hanukkah lights should be kindled. Shammai's school argued that all eight should be lit on the first night and one less each night thereafter, while Hillel's insisted that we start with a single light and add one each night. Eventually, the controversy was resolved in favor of Hillel's school. At first the lamps were separate, but after a while they were combined into a single candlelabrum with nine branches, the extra one being for the shammesh, the candle used to light the others. The hanukiah as we know it is thus reminiscent of the seven-branched menorah used in the Temple at Jerusalem for the Eternal Light. It is still permissible to use single lamps. The only requirement is that each light be distinct, so that there's no confusion about how many have been lit. Electric lights are not allowed, because they are too different from the open flames produced by oil lamps.

When darkness falls and the time comes to light the candles, the family gathers in front of the hanukiah. Whoever is going to perform the ceremony ignites the shammesh and uses it to light the candles, starting on the right with one on the first night, two on the second, and so on until all are lit on the eighth night of the festival. In some families everyone gets a chance to perform the ceremony, including the children. After kindling the hanukiah and pronouncing the blessing, it's customary to sing the hymn "Ma Oz Tzur" ("Rock of Ages"). Then dinner is served.

TRADITIONAL FOODS

Potato pancakes (latkes) and dairy dishes are traditional Hanukkah cuisine. In Israel, a kind of jelly doughnut called sufganiyot is very popular. Usually, however, these foods are served for lunch or as a supper after the games are played, although the non-dairy dishes might be included in the festive dinners ordinarily served throughout the holiday.

POTATO PANCAKES. We serve latkes because it is said that the Maccabee women made pancakes for their husbands on the battlefield. (Any kind of pancake will do, but latkes do not contain milk and therefore are suitable for meat and dairy meals.) Since latkes are cooked in oil, they also remind us of the miraculous oil that lasted eight days. The doughnuts are also fried in oil.

DAIRY FOODS. The custom of eating dairy food derives from the Apocryphal Book of Judith, which has nothing to do with Maccabees revolt but somehow became associated with Hanukkah during the Middle Ages. When a Babylonian general named Holofernes besieged the Judean city of Bethulia, cutting off its water supply, the elders in the city demanded that God make it rain. Appalled by their arrogance, a beautiful widow named Judith decided to do something about the situation. She made her way to Holofernes' tent and seductively gorged him with cheese and wine until he fell asleep. Judith then cut his head off and took it back to Bethulia, where it was displayed on the city gate. When the Babylonian soldiers saw it, they raised the siege and fled.

MENUS

DAIRY LUNCHEON OR SUPPER

Latkes or blintzes, with applesauce or sour cream
Mixed green salad
Sufganiyot, cheese pie, or strudel
Raisins and nuts

DINNER

Lentil soup
Chicken stew
Latkes with apple sauce
Vegetable salad
Sufganiyot
Raisins and nuts

TABLE DECORATION

Since Hanukkah is the Festival of Lights, a lively and meaningful table decoration might be created with hanukiyyot of different designs and candles of different colors. (There's no restriction on how many hanukiyyot you can have in the house or how they're designed, except that the branch for the shammesh should be distinct from the holders for the other candles.) Ornaments representing the holiday might include a hammer (Maccabee probably means hammerer), dreidels, cut-outs of the Hebrew letters on the dreidel, money—either real or candy—and elephants. Elephants? The Greek forces included the giant beasts. Red flowers remind us of the Maccabees' blood shed in the fierce battles, and the blue tablecloth represents the justice of the Jewish cause.

Following are some other ideas for enhancing the festivities with lively and dramatic decorations.

LINENS. Combinations of colorful linens always enliven a table. For a traditional setting, use a white or cream tablecloth with gold or blue napkins, and around the napkins tie contrasting blue or gold ribbons. For a more vibrant and modern effect, use a gold paper tablecloth with red napkins. Or combine a red tablecloth with blue or gold napkins.

HANUKIAH. Make your own oil lamps. It's easy to do. Just pour some olive oil into baby-food jars and submerge about two inches of wick in the oil, with about 1/4 inch above the surface. Arrange eight of them and a candle for the shammesh in a line or circle at the center of the table. (If you have little pitchers or jugs, like those used for pancake syrup, the representation of the original Hanukkah lamps would be even more dramatic.)

ORNAMENTS. In addition to or instead of dreidels, coins, and elephants, appropriate ornaments include:

- Miniature crowns and shields. When Judah and his followers rededicated the Temple, they decorated the outside with crowns and shields.
- Figurines or paper dolls representing the Maccabees (many Jewish gift shops have them).
- Small ceramic pitchers.
- Miniature harps and cymbals (and a zither if you can find one, but that would be difficult).
- Toy hammers.
- Chamsot. A stylized hand, the chamsot is an ancient symbol of fortitude.
- Paper model of the Temple (available in Jewish gift shops).

CHILDREN'S TABLE. Since the festival lasts eight days, there's time to have a party for children and to make it an educational experience. Or when you have guests over for dinner you might want to seat the kids at their own table. As a tablecloth, use a map of Israel. (If you have the time, mark the sites of Maccabee battles with tiny flags or colorful ink. The sites are mentioned in the Books of Maccabees and Josephus' *The Jewish War,* Book 1, as well as in a number of histories of the period.) In the center of the table place a paper model of the Temple. For ornaments use dreidels, small pitchers or jugs, and of course elephants. The children will probably be familiar with the dreidel, but the pitchers and elephants will provide you with an opportunity to tell the story of Hanukkah. Place a coin on each child's napkin.

WALL DECORATIONS. Originally, crowns were garlands of leaves or flowers signifying honorable achievement, and it was probably these that Judah used to decorate the Temple. In any case, real or paper garlands are ideal wall decorations for Hanukkah. Paper chains composed of Stars of David, dreidels, coins, and/or elephants can be draped from photographs or hung on the wall with scotch tape. The story of Judith has been the subject of a number of art works, notably bronzes by Donatello and paintings by Cranach and Vernet. The Maccabee Revolt has also been frequently depicted. Photographs and reproductions of the art are readily available.

GIFTS FOR THE HOST

Art reproduction
Book about Hanukkah
Candles for the hanukiah
Dreidel
Hanukiah
Jelly doughnuts
Map of the Holy Land in the era of the Maccabees
Olive oil
Wine

MEMENTOS FOR GUESTS

Dreidels
Figurines of elephants
Miniature jugs or pitchers
Miniature garlands
Red flowers
Toy hammers

CHECKLIST OF CEREMONIAL AND TRADITIONAL OBJECTS

Hanukiah
Candles
Siddur (prayer book, containing Hanukkah blessings and songs)
Kipots (yarmulkes)
Dreidels
Coins

SUMMARY OF SUGGESTED ORNAMENTS

Art reproductions
Coins (real or candy)
Crowns
Chamsot
Cymbals (miniature)
Dreidels
Elephants (figurines or toys)
Hammer or toy hammers
Harps (miniature)
Hebrew letters
Model of Temple
Map of Israel
Oil lamps
Pitchers or jugs (small)
Red flowers
Shields

RECIPES

POTATO LATKES

Serves 6-8

9 medium potatoes
2 medium onions, minced
3 eggs, slightly beaten
3-4 tbsp. matzo meal (ordinary barley cereal tastes best)
1 tsp. salt
1/8 tsp. pepper
1/2 tsp. baking powder
Salad oil

Wash, peel, and grate potatoes. Place in colander and let stand for 10 minutes, then press out remaining liquid. Mix with onions (the onions may be lightly fried first) and eggs. Add matzo meal, salt, pepper, and baking powder. Mix well. Heat about 1/4 inch of salad oil in a large skillet and add soup-spoonfulls of latke mixture. Fry until golden brown on both sides. Keep in warm oven (180 degrees) until time to serve. Can be made up to a week in advance and frozen. (If not frozen, the potatoes will turn brown.) Reheat in 400 degree oven for 10 minutes. Serve with applesauce, sour cream (or plain yogurt), jam, powdered sugar, or cinnamon.

BLINTZES

Serves 4-8

Batter
2 large eggs
3/4 cup milk
1/2-2/3 cup flour, sifted
Pinch of salt
2 tbsp. margarine, melted

Filling
4 cups creamed cottage cheese
4 tbsp. sour cream
2 egg yolks
3 tbsp. sugar
1/2 tsp. salt
1 tsp. vanilla (optional)

Mix filling ingredients until smooth, then set aside. Mix eggs and milk. Add flour, salt, and margarine while beating until smooth with electric mixer. Coat bottom of 8-inch frying pan with margarine and pour in two tbsp. batter. Tilt pan to spread evenly. Cook over medium heat until just set on top and light gold on bottom. Place bottom side up on cloth or waxed paper, allow to cool slightly, put one or two tbsp. filling in center, and roll up. Fry in margarine until golden brown. If blintzes are not to be served immediately, grease bottoms of baking pans with margarine, put a single layer of blintzes in each, cool, cover tightly, and refrigerate overnight. To serve, reheat from room temperature in 325 degree oven. Top with sour cream, or apple sauce, and powdered sugar, berries, or honey. (Any crepe recipe can be substituted for the batter.)

SUFGANIOT
(Jelly Doughnuts)

Serves 6-8

2 pkgs. dry yeast or 1 oz. compressed yeast
1 3/4 cups milk, hot
2-2 1/2 cups flour
1/4 cup milk, lukewarm
3 eggs
3/4 cup sugar
1 tsp. vanilla
1/2 cup butter or margarine
Jam or jelly (any flavor)
Oil for deep frying
Sugar, powdered or granulated, for coating

Dissolve yeast in lukewarm milk, stir one cup flour into hot milk, combine, and leave in a warm area until bubbly (30-45 minutes). Mix eggs, sugar, and vanilla and add to dough, then add butter and remaining flour. Turn out onto lightly floured board and knead until smooth. Cover with towel, place in warm area, and let rise until doubled in size (about 40 minutes). Roll out to 1/2-inch thickness on floured board and cut into rounds with cookie cutter. Put one tsp. jam between each pair of rounds and press edges together. Cover and let rise for another hour. Drop into hot oil and fry until brown. Drain well, and dust with powdered sugar or dip both sides in granulated sugar.

JELLY DOUGHNUTS
(Alternative) Serves 6-8

2 cups oil
2 cups buttermilk or yogurt
3 1/2 cups self-rising flour
1 tsp. vanilla
4 tbsp. sugar
2 eggs
1/3 tsp. salt
Powdered sugar

Heat the oil in a deep pot. Mix ingredients, except powdered sugar, until dough has smooth texture. Use two spoons to form tablespoon size lumps and drop into hot oil. Fry until golden brown and sprinkle with powdered sugar. Option: Insert jam before frying.

CHEESE PIE

Serves 6

12-oz. carton cream-style cottage cheese
4 eggs, separated
1 cup sugar
Juice of 1 lemon
Pinch of salt
1/2 box of zwieback
1/4 cup margarine
1 tbsp. sugar

Preheat oven to to 350 degrees. Press cheese through sieve (unless using electric mixer) and mix thoroughly with egg yolks, sugar, lemon juice, and salt. Grind zwieback, put into 9-inch pie plate, and pour melted margarine over it. Mix with fork, adding sugar. Press the crumbs in the pan, and pat bottom and sides to form pie crust. Beat egg whites until very stiff, fold into cheese mixture, and pour into crust. Bake for 45-60 minutes. Leave in oven to cool.

STRUDEL
(See recipes for the Sabbath.)

LENTIL SOUP

Serves 6-8

1 cup lentils
2 medium onions, diced
1 celery heart, diced
1 bay leaf
1 1/2 quarts water
Salt and pepper to taste
3 tbsp. tomato paste or 1/4 cup salsa
2 tbsp. white wine vinegar
Oil (olive or salad) for sauteing

Wash lentils, cover with cold water, soak for two hours, and drain. Saute onions and celery in soup pot until transparent. Add lentils, water, bay leaf, salt, pepper, and tomato paste or salsa. Bring to boil, cover, and simmer for 1 to 1 1/2 hours. Add vinegar, adjust seasoning if necessary, and simmer for additional half hour.

CHICKEN STEW

Serves 4

Whole chicken, cut up, or 4 chicken breasts
2 small cloves garlic, mashed
2 medium onions, diced
1 can tomatoes, chopped
1 large green pepper, sliced
2 tbsp. pimento, chopped
2 tbsp. parsley, minced
1/2 tsp. thyme
1/2 tsp. oregano
1/4 tsp. pepper
2/3 cup dry white wine
2 cups fresh mushrooms, thinly sliced

Place ingredients in large pot, cover, and simmer for 1 1/2 hours.

CHAPTER 6
Tu Be Shevat
(Shevat 15: January or February)

When you come to the land [of Israel] and have planted all manner of trees for food, then you shall count the fruit thereof as forbidden; three years shall it be as forbidden to you; it shall not be eaten. And in the fourth year all the fruit thereof shall be holy, for giving praise unto the Lord. But in the fifth year you may eat the fruit thereof, that it may yield unto you more richly the increase thereof.

Leviticus 19:23-24

Although Tu Be Shevat is a minor holiday and is not mentioned in the Bible, it has become important for the development of the modern state of Israel. On that day school children and their teachers plant trees, and Jews living in other countries donate money for the activity. As a result, thousands of acres of land denuded by centuries of neglect and erosion have been reforested.

The holiday was established in the Mishna, which declared the 15th of Shevat (Tu means 15 in Hebrew) to be the new year for trees. It's about this time of the year in the Holy Land that the winter rains cease and the sap begins to rise in plants. (Inevitably, a legend developed regarding Tu Be Shevat: It is said that God decides on that day which plants will flourish during the year, just as He decides on Yom Kippur who will live and who will die.) In the Talmudic commentaries, the rabbis wrote that it is mandatory for the Jewish people to plant trees in their land.

Trees connote the Creation and eternal hope—the Garden of Eden, the Tree of Life. At the time of the Second Temple, couples would proudly celebrate the birth of a child by planting a tree—a cedar for a boy, a cypress for a girl—and the custom has endured in Israel to the present time. In his lovely poem "On Tu Be Shevat," S. Shalom tells about an angel who writes the names of all the plants in a notebook. When the book is full, the desert will bloom like a garden and the messiah will appear.

Devotion to nature and by implication protection of the environment reflect the spirit of the festival. The colors of the day are, of course, green and brown.

TRADITIONAL FOODS

Despite the fact that Tu Be Shevat is not, strictly speaking, a religious holiday, Jews living in the Diaspora used to celebrate it with a festive meal to testify that their spiritual roots remained in the soil of the Holy Land. The meal was based on the beautiful description of Israel in Deuteronomy (8:7-9): "For the Lord your God brings you into a good land, a land of brooks and fountains, of springs welling up in valleys and hills; a land of wheat and barley, and vines and fig trees, and pomegranates; a land of olive trees and honey; a land where you shall eat bread without scarceness." At a minimum the meal included the seven foods mentioned in Deuteronomy (the term honey meant date juice). Almonds were also served, because they were thought to be the first trees to blossom in Israel. Carob—a very sweet and fibrous fruit—became popular, since it grows abundantly in that part of the world. (The custom of eating carob was fortified by a legend. Simon Bar Yochai, the story goes, refused to submit to a Roman decree against teaching the Torah. Threatened with arrest, he hid in a cave, where he subsisted on the fruit.) Wealthy people put fifteen types of fruit on the table, signifying the 15th of Shevat, and some villages would serve a communal meal featuring a wide variety of produce. Since it was not possible to plant trees in Israel, the custom developed of giving 91 cents to charity. The amount is the sum of the numbers represented by the letters in the Hebrew word for tree, *ilan.*

Then in the sixteenth century, the mystical Cabalists introduced a more ritualistic Tu Be Shevat meal fashioned after the Passover seder. During the ceremony, participants eat various combinations of fruits and nuts, which are divided into three categories. In the first group are ten fruits that are entirely edible, such as grapes and figs. The second group includes ten fruits with pits. And the third consists of ten nuts and fruits that have inedible skins, like pomegranates. Edible parts of the foods symbolize holiness, the inedible pits stand for impurity, and the shells protect the holiness. Traditionalist families still conduct the seder, but others simply get together to affirm their devotion to Jewish nationhood by eating fruits and nuts borne by the trees that grow in Israel. Dried or canned fruits and packaged nuts may be used when fresh ones are not available.

Fruits and nuts that grow in Israel include:

Almond	Lime
Apple	Loquat
Apricot	Mulberry
Banana	Olive
Cantaloupe	Orange
Carob	Peach
Citron	Pear
Date	Pinenut
Fig	Plum
Grape	Pomegranate
Grapefruit	Quince
Hazelnut	Strawberry
Honeydew melon	Walnut
Lemon	Watermelon

MENU

Tray of fruit, or bowls of different fruits
Green salad, with black and green olives and sprinkled nuts
Roast chicken, with fruit, walnut, and onion stuffing
Rice with almonds, or barley ring
Broccoli with pine nuts
Stuffed dates
Apple pie, brandied fruit balls, or carrot-pineapple cake
Wine
Pomegranate-orangeade

TABLE DECORATION

The fruit itself becomes the mainstay of your Tu Be Shevat table decoration. On a brown or white tablecloth, place baskets or bowls (preferably clay) of different fruits and nuts. Embellish the fruit theme with tree branches (if you can find one from a blossoming almond tree, that would be ideal). You might add toy birds, for as a traditional Israeli children's song, "The Almond Trees are White," says:

> The almond trees are white,
> The sun is shining bright
> Singing birds from every dome
> Tell us Tu Be Shevat has come,
> The holiday of the trees.

Suitable alternative decorations include:

LINENS. Instead of brown linens, use pink and white because they are the colors of almond blossoms. Or combine brown, pink, and white, perhaps using place mats or runners.

CENTERPIECES. Arrange the fruits and nuts on a large tray in the center of the table, and surround the trays with branches—from blossoming trees, if possible. Or create a centerpiece out of a toy bank or jewel box for collecting charity donations. Surround it with branches and pieces of fruit.

ENTERTAINING ON THE JEWISH HOLIDAYS

ORNAMENTS. In addition to the birds, some appropriate ornaments are

- Small potted plants
- Planting tools
- Framed photographs of Israeli arbors and vineyards
- Vases of twigs with white-and-pink cotton balls attached. (You create the pink by dabbing red ink on the cotton. Attach the balls to the twigs with glue or scotch tape.)
- Cardboard trees
- Charity box (when not used as centerpiece)

GIFTS FOR THE HOST

Certificate for tree to be planted in host's name (can be purchased at most synagogues)

Dry fruit
Fruitcake
Fruit candy
Plant
Planting tools
Wine

MEMENTOS FOR GUESTS

Basket (miniature) of raisins and nuts
Bird (paper or plastic)
Clay pot (miniature) filled with stuffed dates or other small desserts

SUMMARY OF SUGGESTED ORNAMENTS

Birds
Branches
Charity box
Photographs of Israeli arbors and vineyards
Planting tools
Plants
Vases of twigs and cotton balls

RECIPES

STUFFED CHICKEN

Serves 4-6

One 3-5-lb. chicken, prepared for stuffing
1 large or 2 small onions
6 oz. dried apricots or prunes, or combination
1/4 cup walnuts, chopped
Salt to taste
Paprika to taste
White wine (optional)

Preheat oven to 350 degrees. Rub chicken with salt inside and out. Slice onions, saute briefly, add fruit, saute until it and the onions are soft, add walnuts, and stuff into chicken. Sprinkle with paprika and roast until leg moves freely when pulled away from body of chicken (about 1 1/4 to 1 3/4 hours, depending on weight of bird). (Stuffing can also be used with turkey or duckling.) If desired, baste occasionally with white wine.

RICE WITH ALMONDS

Serves 4-6

1 cup long-grain white or brown rice
1/2 cup almonds, sliced
1 tsp. sesame seeds
2 tsp. margarine
2 cups chicken broth
1/4 tsp. salt
Black pepper to taste

Spread almonds and sesame seeds on cookie sheet or aluminum foil. Roast in 350 degree oven until golden brown (10-15 minutes), shaking occasionally. Melt margarine in a deep skillet and saute rice until golden brown. Mix in nuts, add chicken broth, salt, and pepper. Bring to boil, then reduce heat, cover tightly, and simmer very slowly until liquid is absorbed (20-25 minutes). Fluff with fork and replace cover until ready to serve.

BARLEY RING

Serves 4

1 cup barley
1 cup celeriac (celery root), peeled and diced
1 cup carrots, diced
2 tsp. salt (more or less)
Generous pinch mint and/or basil

Preheat oven to 350 degrees. Put diced vegetables into two quarts rapidly boiling salted water. Remove after one minute. Add barley to boiling water, remove from heat after two minutes, and drain. Mix vegetables, barley, mint/basil, and salt to taste. Place in a well-oiled ring mold (if teflon lined, use very little oil or parve margarine). Bake for 30-40 minutes. Serve hot or cold.

BROCCOLI WITH PINE NUTS

Serves 6-8

3 lbs. fresh broccoli
1/3 cup olive or vegetable oil
1/2 cup pine nuts
2 cloves garlic, minced
1/2 cup water
Salt and pepper to taste

Remove broccoli florets from stems, peel stems and cut in half lengthwise. If thick, cut crosswise into 1/2 inch thick slices. Plunge florets and stems into a large pot filled with boiling salted water and cook for four minutes. Refresh under cold running water, and drain on paper towels. Pour oil into frying pan, brown pine nuts lightly, add garlic, and saute for 30 seconds. Remove nuts and garlic, and put the broccoli in the pan. Toss gently over moderate heat for two minutes, then add water and cook over high heat for six minutes or until water has evaporated and broccoli is tender. Mix in pine nuts and garlic, salt, and pepper. Serve hot.

STUFFED PITTED DATES

1 box pitted dates
Almonds, or walnuts, or dried fruit and nuts mixed with orange juice
Powdered sugar (optional)

Insert half a walnut or a whole almond into each date. Or chop a handful of dried apricots, raisins, and nuts, mix with one tbsp. orange juice, and stuff into dates. Dates may be rolled in powdered sugar before serving.

APPLE PIE

Serves 6-8

19-inch baked pie shell

Filling
1 tbsp. corn starch
1/2 cup sugar
1/4 cup heavy cream (whipping cream)
1 1/4-lb. can sliced apples, well drained
3 tbsp. butter
1 tbsp. lemon juice
1/2 tsp. nutmeg
1/4 tsp. salt

Combine cornstarch and sugar in saucepan, add cream, stir, and place over medium heat until boiling (keep stirring, otherwise the mixture will burn). Add apples and simmer for 10 minutes. Add butter, lemon juice, and spices. When cool, spoon into crust.

Topping
One 8-oz. pkg. cream cheese
1/3 cup sugar
1 egg
1/2 cup coconut, grated
1/2 cup walnuts, chopped

Beat cream cheese, sugar, and egg until fluffy, and spoon over filling. Sprinkle with coconut and walnuts.

BRANDIED FRUIT BALLS

Serves 15-20

2 1/2 cups vanilla wafer crumbs (about 65 wafers, crumbled)
14-oz. can sweetened condensed mincemeat
1 1/4 cup chopped nuts
1/3 cup candied cherries, chopped
2 tbsp. cocoa or chocolate
1 1/2 oz. brandy, or more to taste
1/2-1 cup powdered sugar or flaked coconut

Mix all the ingredients, except the sugar or coconut, in a large bowl until thoroughly blended. Wet hands so mixture does not stick, and form into small balls—about one tbsp. each. Coat balls with sugar or coconut, and place on platter or baking sheet lined with waxed paper. Refrigerate until firm (about two hours). Keep in refrigerator until served and if any are left over.

CARROT-PINEAPPLE CAKE
(See Chapter 3, Rosh Hashanah)

POMEGRANATE-ORANGEADE

Serves 2-3

Mix juice of one pomegranate with that of two oranges. Add an equal amount of sparkling water.

CHAPTER 7

Purim
(Adar 14: February or March)

Mordecai . . . sent letters to all the Jews in all the provinces of King Ahasuerus, near and far, to establish this among them, that they should keep the fourteenth day of the month Adar, and the fifteenth day of the same, every year, as the days when the Jews rested from their enemies, and the month in which their sorrow was turned into joy, and mourning into a good day; that they should make them days of feasting and joy, and of sending portions to each other, and gifts to the poor.

Esther 9:20-22

Of all the festivals in the Jewish calendar, the most exuberant and fun-filled is Purim. In Israel it is celebrated with parades in which everyone wears costumes and masks and is well-soused in accordance with the Talmud's instructions to be so drunk on Purim that you can't tell the difference between "Blessed be Mordecai" and "Cursed be Haman." The celebration is similar to the Mardi Gras carnival.

Purim commemorates the story of Esther and Mordecai's deliverance of the Jews of Persia from the massacre ordered by the evil Haman. Many scholars contend that the Biblical Book of Esther, in which the story is told, is a work of fiction written centuries after the events supposedly occurred. Whether or not they're correct, the book expresses a profound truth: the endurance and ultimate triumph of the Jewish people despite the many attempts over the centuries to annihilate us.

The Book of Esther tells how King Ahasuerus (probably Xerxes I, 486-465 B.C.E., or Artaxerxes II, 404-359) became enraged when his wife Queen Vashti disobeyed his order to appear at a banquet and "show the people and the princes her beauty." On the advice of his wise men, who warned that her disobedience could be a bad example to other women, he deposed Vashti. After holding a sort of beauty contest, the king selected Esther (Hadassah) to be his queen, not knowing she was Jewish.

Sometime later, Esther's foster-father Mordecai, who worked for the government, learned of a plot against Ahasuerus, informed Esther of it, and she in turn warned the king. Mordecai's deed was inscribed in the official chronicles. But then Ahasuerus appointed a new grand vizier named Haman, who asserted his authority by demanding that government employees bow down to him. Mordecai refused. Furious, Haman wreaked vengeance on Mordecai by obtaining the king's permission to kill all the Jews in his domain. To determine the most propitious day for the massacre, lots (purim, in Hebrew) were cast, and Adar 14 was chosen.

When Mordecai learned about this, he put on sackcloth and ashes and went through the city, wailing loudly and bitterly. Esther sent her chamberlain to find out why Mordecai was so upset, and he sent back a message that the queen should go to the king and plead with him in behalf of her people. She replied, however, that anyone who approached the king in the inner court without having been summoned by him could be put to death and it had been thirty days since he had called for her. Mordecai sent back a message, saying "Don't think that just because you live in the king's palace you're going to be the only Jew who escapes the edict." Resigned, Esther asked Mordecai to bid the Jewish community in Susa, where the edict was first promulgated, to fast three days for her, then she'd go to the king. "If I perish, I perish."

Clearly, Ahasuerus still loved his wife, because he welcomed her and promised to grant any request she made, "even if it's half my kingdom." She was clever, though, and invited him and Haman to a banquet. At the banquet the king again asked her what she wanted, and Esther invited him and Haman to another banquet, at which she would make her request. Haman was so flattered at being the only one invited to the banquet with the king that he was in high spirits all day, until he saw Mordecai, who refused to stand up when he approached or give any other sign of recognition. On the advice of his wife and friends, he decided to ask the king's permission to hang Mordecai, and had a gallows built for the purpose.

That night Ahasuerus was unable to sleep, so he had the official chronicles read to him and came across the entry about Mordecai's discovery of the plot against the king. Ahasuerus asked whether Mordecai had ever received a reward for what he did, and the king was told that nothing had been done for him. He decided to rectify the situation. At that very moment Haman entered the king's anti-chamber, intending to request permission to hang Mordecai. The king had him brought in, and asked him what in his opinion would be the right way to treat a man whom the king wanted to honor. Haman, thinking Ahasuerus was talking about him, replied: "Have servants bring royal robes that the king has worn and a horse that he's ridden, with a royal diadem on its head. Then have the noblest of the king's officers put the robes on the man and lead him on horseback along the main street of the city, proclaiming that this is the way to treat a man whom the king wants to honor." Ahasuerus then ordered Haman to honor Mordecai just that way. Haman did as he was told, then complained miserably to his wife about what had happened. She foresaw that this was the beginning of the end for Haman. While they were talking, the king's servants arrived to conduct Haman to Esther's banquet.

At the banquet Ahasuerus again asked Esther for her request, again promising even half his kingdom if that's what she wanted. "If I have found favor in your eyes, O King," she replied, "and if it please the king, grant me my life, that is what I request, and I request the lives of my people. For we are condemned, I and my people, to be destroyed, to be slain, to perish. If we had been handed over to become slaves, I would have held my tongue, but the enemy will be unable to make good the loss to the king from what is about to happen." The king asked who was responsible for this, and Esther told him it was Haman. In a rage, Ahasuerus went out into the garden, and the terrified Haman begged Esther to save his life. When the king returned, he found Haman leaning over the queen's couch and thought the grand vizier was about to violate his wife. Ahasuerus then condemned Haman to be hanged on the gallows he built for Mordecai's execution. When he learned that Mordecai was Esther's foster-father, the king gave him Haman's job. Esther then asked Ahasuerus to reverse Haman's edict for the massacre of the Jews. He instructed Mordecai to write to the rulers of the various provinces and to the Jews in every city, granting the Jews the right to defend themselves against anyone who attacked them, effective Adar 13. On that day the Jews in most provinces defeated their enemies, and on Adar 14 celebrated their victory with feasts. In the walled town of Shushan, the fighting lasted from the thirteenth to the fourteenth, and the victory celebration was held on the fifteenth.

Mordecai subsequently instructed the Jews to commemorate the events every year. On the thirteenth we fast in remembrance of the fast requested by Esther before she approached the king. The next day is a general celebration, and in walled towns—which in our time primarily means Jerusalem—the rejoicing extends to the fifteenth, called Shushan Purim. Mordecai also ordered the celebrants to send portions of food to each other and give gifts to the poor.

The entire Book of Esther is read aloud in the synagogue on the morning of Adar 14 and again in the evening. To the utter delight of the children, they are encouraged to participate by twirling gragers, clashing cymbals, tooting horns, and otherwise making ear-shattering noise every time Haman's name is mentioned. Then in the afternoon families get together, often with friends, for a leisurely, bibulous, and sometimes raucous meal, the Purim seudah (the word means banquet or festive meal). Vivid colors like red, yellow, and purple reflect the mood of the boisterous and thoroughly enjoyable celebration—but black, too, because it represents the evil Haman.

TRADITIONAL OBJECTS AND FOODS

Since Purim is not a Torah holiday, but a commemorative one, ceremonial objects used at the Purim seudah and the foods served are sanctified by custom instead of law.

MEGILLA.   For the Purim ceremonies at home and in the synagogue, the Book of Esther is inscribed on a megilla, or scroll, and is read like a letter to replicate the way decrees and other official communications were dispatched in ancient Persia. Since God is never referred to directly in the book, the megilla may be elaborately decorated, unlike the Torah scroll and megillas for other books in the Bible.

GRAGER.   A rattle that produces a sharp clacking sound, the grager is the customary instrument for making noise when Haman's name is pronounced. Cymbals and horns are also used sometimes. The tradition of making noise has its roots in the ancient folk belief that loud and harsh sounds scare away evil spirits.

KIDDUSH CUP.   While kiddush is not recited at the seudah because Purim is not based on the Torah, it is customary to say something nonsensical over the kiddush cup. The parody of the kiddush is characteristic of the topsy-turvy hilarity of the Purim celebration.

MASKS.   At many seudahs the celebrants wear masks, and they might even don costumes. The tradition may have developed from the influence of European Mardi Gras carnivals, but undoubtedly has its source in the folk belief that disguise is protection from sinister forces. (If you don't have masks, sunglasses will do.)

HAMANTASCH. Meaning "pocket of Haman," the hamantasch (plural: hamantaschen) is a three-cornered pastry filled with poppy-seeds, prunes, or other fruit. Originally, it was a German pastry called mohntasch, "pocket of poppy seeds." A tradition developed among European Jews that the triangular shape represents the three-cornered hat presumably worn by Haman.

KREPLACH. Triangular kreplach—meat-filled dough—is also a popular Purim dish, for much the same reason as hamentaschen.

MENU

> *Cucumber soup*
> *Kreplach or dolmas*
> *Couscous with meat and vegetables, or*
> *chicken in wine with white rice*
> *Tomato salad*
> *Hamantasch*
> *Fruit dipped in chocolate*
> *Wine*

TABLE DECORATION

The Purim story lends itself to dramatization, and in some households the seudah is preceded by skits based on the tale. (For a girl with theatrical aspirations, the part of Esther is a superb opportunity to display her talent.) Whether or not you turn your dining room into a theater, you can create a dramatic tableau by decorating the table and walls with masks. Round out the decoration with symbols like a horse (representing Mordecai's triumphant ride), three-cornered hats (representing Haman) made out of paper, and perhaps a megilla. Be sure to give everyone something to make noise with.

There are many other possibilities for dramatic decorations. For example:

LINENS.

- If your tablecloth is white, cut black gift paper into triangles and use them as place mats on top of the linen. Also use black paper napkins, folded into triangles.

- A red tablecloth with black place mats and napkins would be even more dramatic.

- For a harlequin effect, use a polka-dot tablecloth and domino (eye) masks as napkin rings.

CENTERPIECES.

- Surround a three-cornered hat with gragers and other noisemakers, such as toy drums, clackers, triangles, rattles, cymbals, and horns. (You can make a hat very easily out of stiff paper. Just fold a square or rectangular sheet of paper in half. Then

fold down the two corners of the closed edge to form a triangle. Fold up the strips remaining on the bottom—and you have a hat.)

- On the head of a toy horse place a diadem (you can make it out of a little strip of gold paper, and on its back place a male doll in a gold cloak (a piece of cloth or crepe paper). Use another doll—preferably an ugly one—to represent Haman leading the horse.

- Fill a large bowl with hamantaschen, and surround it with colored candles.

TABLE ORNAMENTS.

- Black triangles pasted on a white tablecloth.

- Domino (eye) masks.

- Miniature megillas.

- Tiny black three-cornered hats.

- Miniature noisemakers.

- Figurines of Esther, Mordecai, Ahasuerus, Haman, and Vashti.

- Stars of David.

- Miniature crowns.

- Flowers with black ribbons.

- Clown hats.

- Sunglasses.

CHILDREN'S TABLE.   Cover the table with a purple or black paper tablecloth, and in the center place a paper horse filled with candy. (Let them break it open after dinner.) Paste pictures of Esther, Mordecai, and Ahasuerus on the tablecloth, or mount them on cardboard frames. On each child's plate put a noisemaker and a miniature megilla. Give everyone a gold crown to wear, and scatter tiny three-cornered hats around the table.

GIFTS
(Mishloah Manot)

Because Mordecai ordered us to send portions of our feast to each other on Purim, it is customary to give relatives and friends plates of food. The practice is called mishloah manot (sending gifts). In Israel and Jewish neighborhoods elsewhere, the goodies are often delivered by children dressed in costumes and wearing masks. Guests at a seudah bring a plate of food with them and leave with another plateful (not infrequently exchanging more or less the same things). The usual foods, and a few unusual ones, include:

Hamantaschen
Wine (a split is enough)

Small cakes and pies
Fruit
Nuts
Candy
Pickled vegetables
Preserves, jellies, jams
Salami sticks

CHECK LIST OF TRADITIONAL OBJECTS AND FOODS

Megilla of Esther
Gragers and other noisemakers
Kiddush cup
Masks
Hamantaschen
Kreplach
Kipots (yarmulkes)

SUMMARY OF SUGGESTED ORNAMENTS

Black triangles
Clacker
Clown hats
Crowns (miniature)
Cymbal
Drum (toy)
Figurines of Esther, Mordecai, Ahasuerus, Haman,
    and Vashti
Flowers with black ribbons
Grager
Horn
Horse
Masks
Megilla (miniature)
Rattle
Stars of David
Sunglasses
Three-cornered hat (miniature)
Triangle

RECIPES

CUCUMBER SOUP

Serves 4-6

2 lbs. peeled cucumbers, cut into 1/2-inch pieces
4 tbsp. oil or parve margarine
1/2 cup green onion, chopped fine
7-8 cups chicken broth
2 tsp. wine vinegar
1-2 tsp. dried dill weed or 3 tsp. fresh, minced
6 tbsp. farina breakfast cereal
Salt and white pepper to taste
1/4 cup walnuts, chopped fine

Place the oil or margarine in a two quart pot, heat, add onions, and cook, while stirring over medium heat for about one minute or until onions are opaque. Do not brown. Add cucumbers, chicken broth, vinegar, and dill. Bring to boil, then slowly add the cereal while stirring continuously. Reduce heat to simmer and cook, uncovered, for 20 minutes or until cereal is well cooked. Stir from time to time to prevent sticking. Allow soup to cool slightly, then put through mill or mix in food processor until smooth. If very thick, thin with one or two tbsp. chicken broth to desired consistency. Add salt and white pepper to taste. Serve hot or cold, sprinkled with chopped walnuts. Can be kept in freezer for several weeks.

KREPLACH
(See Chapter 3, Rosh Hashanah.)

DOLMAS
(Stuffed Grape Leaves)

Serves 6-8

1 jar grape leaves
1 lb. ground beef or turkey
2 garlic cloves, minced
2 large onions, chopped fine
1/2 cup pine nuts or walnuts, chopped fine
1/4 cup mushrooms, diced
Salt, black pepper, and paprika to taste
1/2 cup olive oil, plus 1 tbsp.

Mix meat with garlic, salt, pepper, and paprika. Saute in 1/2 tbsp. olive oil until lightly browned. Remove from heat and scrape mixture into a large mixing bowl. Add 1/2 tbsp. olive oil to pan and fry onions until golden and opaque. Add chopped nuts and mushrooms, stir and fry a little longer, then mix with meat. Preheat oven to 350 degrees.

Remove grape leaves from jar, saving the liquid. Separate each leaf and gently flatten, being careful not to tear, and spread on wax paper. Place one tsp. of meat mixture on each leaf lengthwise, roll into packets, and tuck in the ends. Place in layers in a medium-size casserole, mix juice from jar of grape leaves with 1/2 cup olive oil, and pour it over the packets. Add enough water to cover. Bake for 1/2 hour, adding a little water as needed to prevent drying out.

COUSCOUS

Serves 8

2 pkgs. couscous, prepared according to directions on package
2 lbs. beef, lamb, or chicken, cut into 1- to 2-in. cubes
1/4 cup olive oil
5 large carrots, peeled
2 large yellow onions
1 small cabbage
3 zucchini
3 medium tomatoes
10 cups water
1/4 cup canned garbanzo beans
1/2 tsp. parsley, minced
1/2 tsp. cilantro, minced
1/2 cup raisins (optional)

Put meat, olive oil, carrots, onions, cabbage, zucchini, tomatoes, and water in large pot and bring to a boil. Cover, and simmer for 1 1/4 hours or until meat is tender. During the last 15 minutes, add parsley, cilantro, and garbanzo beans. (Add raisins, if used.) With a slotted spoon, remove the meat and vegetables from the liquid. To serve in the traditional manner, put a few tablespoons of couscous on each plate, pour about a spoonful of the liquid over it, and place pieces of meat and vegetables on top. Alternatively, take the couscous, liquid, meat, and vegetables to the table in separate serving bowls. The mixture may also be served on a large platter with the couscous on the bottom and the meat and vegetables in layers on top. Garnish with parsley.

CHICKEN IN WINE

Serves 4-6

1 chicken, cut up
2 tbsp. salad oil
2 tbsp. margarine
2 large onions, chopped
2 cups mushrooms, diced
2 cloves garlic, minced
Salt and pepper to taste
1 cup dry red wine

Saute onions in half the oil and margarine until golden. Remove onions from pan and set aside. Add more oil and margarine to the pan. Mix flour, salt, and pepper and coat the chicken pieces. Fry until golden brown. Remove from frying pan and place in a large pot, add onions, mushrooms, garlic, and a little more salt and pepper, and pour wine over all. Cook over low heat until fork tender (20-30 minutes). If the liquid is too thin, thicken the sauce with a little flour or cornstarch.

TOMATO SALAD

Serves 4

2 large tomatoes
2 large cucumbers

Slice tomatoes and cucumbers into thin rounds and arrange in overlapping circles on a platter. Garnish with parsley and ladle dressing over the top.

Dressing
1/2 cup lightly toasted sesame seeds
4 tbsp. wine vinegar
1 tbsp. sugar
Salt and pepper to taste (optional)

Mix the ingredients thoroughly with a wire whisk or in a blender before using.

HAMANTASCHEN

Serves 40

4 cups regular white flour
4 eggs
4 tsp. baking soda
1/2-3/4 cup vegetable oil
3/4 cup sugar

Filling
1 1/2 cups poppy seed
1 cup whole milk or parve non-dairy cream
1 tbsp. butter or margarine
4 tbsp. honey
5 tbsp. sugar
2 tsp. lemon juice

Boil the milk with the sugar, Poppy seeds, and butter. Reduce heat and simmer until the milk is absorbed. Add the remaining ingredients, mix well, simmer a few minutes, and remove from heat. Set aside and allow to cool.

Sift the flour, baking soda, and sugar together into a large bowl. Add the oil and eggs and mix thoroughly. Knead until the ingredients hold together and the dough is formed, roll out to 1/2-in. thickness on a floured board. Cut into rounds using a mug or tea cup as a cookie cutter. Pinch the edges tightly at three corners forming a triangle, and to prevent the filling from leaking out. Put a teaspoonful of filling in the center of each cookie. (If Poppy seeds are not available, fill the Hamantaschen with any flavor of jam desired.) Place the Hamantaschen on a cookie sheet, separated so the edges do not touch, and bake in preheated 350-degree oven approximately 30–35 minutes until the cookies are golden. Remove from oven and let cool before serving.

CHOCOLATE DIPPED FRUIT
(Parve)

Dried fruit or fresh strawberries, sliced bananas, pineapple spears, or kiwi slices
Parve sweetened chocolate bar or chips

Cover a baking sheet or a large tray with waxed paper. Put chocolate bar, broken into pieces, or the chips in the top of a double boiler, and place over moderate heat. As soon as the chocolate begins to melt, stir until smooth and liquefied. Remove pot from heat. Dip each piece of fruit into chocolate, coating half of each side, and place on waxed paper. Cool until firm enough to handle, and then dip other side of the fruit in the chocolate. If the chocolate becomes lumpy, add oil, a few drops at a time, until the mixture is smooth. Refrigerate until chocolate sets and fruit is firm enough to handle. (Make enough to serve several pieces to each person.)

CHAPTER 8

Passover
(Nisan 14–21: March or April)

In the first month, on the fourteenth day of the month at dusk, is the Lord's passover. And on the fifteenth day of the same month is the feast of unleavened bread unto the Lord; seven days you shall eat unleavened bread.

Leviticus 23:5-6

A vivid picture of what the first night of Passover must have been like at the time of the Second Temple was painted by a historian of the Jewish holidays: "Towards evening [after the Paschal sacrifice] thousands of Jews rush from the Mount of the Temple through the streets of Jerusalem, each bearing on his shoulder the sacrificial animal wrapped in its own skin. All are busy and expectant, preparing themselves for the great night of the year, the night of redemption. Darkness descends upon the city. Everywhere sheep and goats, spitted on fragrant pomegranate wood, are roasting in the clay stoves which stand in the courtyards of the homes. . . . The groups are now gathering. Relatives and friends assemble from near and far. Every large room is a meeting place for a group. Nobody is omitted. The poor are invited to the homes of the rich and a spirit of brotherliness, of national unity, binds all together in a feast. All are partners—masters and slaves, men and women, the aged and the youthful. The celebration begins."*

And the celebration has changed very little since then. The first night of Passover is still the highlight of our year, a night for reunions with family and friends, when we commemorate the redemption of the Jewish people. While in the days of the Second Temple the celebrants probably lounged on sofas spread around the room, we gather around the table and recount, as they did, the story of our ancestors' escape from Egypt and the birth of Jewish nationhood. Like our ancestors, we eat matzo, taste bitter herbs, and partake of the sacrificial lamb. The only major differences are that we now have the Haggadah to guide us through the ceremony, we no longer sacrifice animals, and we place a glass of wine on the table for Elijah. Scholars disagree about whether four glasses of wine were drunk at the time of the Second Temple or whether the tradition was introduced later.

Various Jewish communities have added their own customs to the observance. In some, for example, participants in the seder wear white clothes, symbolizing God's justice and mercy. Tunisians eat their meat very quickly while sitting on the floor, to reenact the hasty meal eaten by Israelites before they fled from Egypt. In many European families everyone receives a new outfit. At Sephardic seders everyone at the table joins in reading the

---

*Hayyim Schauss, *The Jewish Festivals* (Cincinnati: Union of American Hebrew Congregations, 1938), p. 54.

87

Haggadah, whereas in Ashkenazi households only the leader of the ceremony reads it, except for the four questions asked by the youngest person.

In Israel the Passover festival lasts seven days, but is extended to eight in some Diaspora communities. The extra day was added because of uncertainties about the Jewish calendar and reliance upon information sent from Jerusalem by messenger. Since the holiday must last seven days, it was necessary to allow enough time in case the messenger arrived late. Thus arose the custom of holding a seder on the second, as well as the first, night of Passover.

The festival is known by four names:

(1) *PASSOVER (Pesach* in Hebrew), because the Angel of Death passed over the homes of the Israelites when striking down the first-born in Egypt. During that terrible night Pharaoh summoned Moses and agreed to let the Israelites leave Egypt. We celebrate these events on the first night of Passover.

(2) *FEAST OF UNLEAVENED BREAD (Chag-hamatzot),* in commemoration of the faith of the Israelites in God when they fled their homes with nothing to eat but hastily baked bread.

(3) *SEASON OF OUR LIBERATION (Zman Cheiruteinu),* which refers specifically to our struggle for freedom in Egypt but also encompasses our continuing fight throughout the ages to remain free.

(4) *SPRING FESTIVAL (Chag Ha-aviv),* in celebration of the annual reflowering of nature. It symbolizes eternal hope and the rebirth of the Israelites when they entered the promised land. The arrival of spring was celebrated by the Israelites long before the deliverance from Egypt, and the festival merged with Passover.

In spirit, the Passover holiday is thus joyous, optimistic, and profoundly affirmative. Traditional colors are white (symbolizing purity), blue (love of divine works), and purple (justice). But bright spring colors are equally appropriate—green, yellow, pink.

CEREMONIAL FOODS AND OBJECTS

The seder held on the first night of Passover, and often repeated on the second by families living in the diaspora, is the principal ceremony of the festival. Matzo, bitter herbs (maror), wine, and a copy of the Haggadah are essential for the ceremony—without them there cannot be a seder. Other foods and objects, though, have long been part of the Passover tradition and should be provided.

FOODS

MATZO. Made simply of flour and water, without leaven or salt. Three pieces are stacked on a plate and covered by a napkin (or placed in a special cloth matzo holder with three pockets). They symbolize the ancient division of the Jewish nation into Kohanim (priests), Levites, and Israelites. The middle one is broken in two unequal parts by the leader of the ceremony, who wraps the larger part in a napkin and sets it aside or, if a child is present, hides it. Called the afikomen, from the Greek word for dessert, it is tasted by everyone at the end of the meal and represents the sacrificial lamb. Hiding the afikomen is a customary device for keeping children awake during the long evening. The one who finds it receives a gift. A number of ancient superstitions about the powers of the afikomen are tenaciously believed to this day. For example, some Iranian and Afghan Jews keep pieces in their homes as protection against the evil eye. Credulous pregnant women hold it during delivery to bring them good luck.

MAROR. Bitter herbs, which remind us of the bitterness of slavery. Maror usually consists of romaine (cos) lettuce or unsweetened horseradish, preferably freshly ground. Endive or escarole may be used instead.

CHAROSET. A pasty mixture of chopped nuts and fruit— usually apples—cinnamon or a similar spice, and wine. It is eaten with the maror. Charoset stands for the mortar used by the Israelites in the construction of Egyptian buildings.

Z'ROAH. A bone, traditionally lamb shank or shoulder blade, representing the paschal lamb. It is roasted until the outside is charred, or after roasting it can be held over an open flame.

BEITZAH. Roasted or hard-boiled egg, symbolizing the sacrificial offering at the Temple, but also the cycle of life and the springtime renewal of the earth.

KARPAS. Parsley or other vegetable, preferably green. It represents spring.

SALT WATER. Used for dipping the Karpas in commemoration of the tears of slavery.

WINE. Grape juice or another fruit juice may be substituted. The four glasses drunk recall God's promises to take the Israelites out of Egypt, serve them, redeem them, and lead them to the Promised Land.

OBJECTS

SEDER PLATE. Centerpiece of the table, contains portions of all the ceremonial foods, except the saltwater and wine. The matzo is sometimes placed in the center, with the other foods around it. Ordinarily, though, it's separate. Any plate may be used, but many families own special ones made of glass, porcelain, silver, copper, or some other fine material and beautifully designed. Food on the plate is not eaten. Each celebrant receives individual portions, along with salt water.

ELIJAH'S CUP. A cup of wine set aside for the prophet. Any goblet may be used, but usually it's large, made of precious metal, and elaborately decorated. The custom of pouring a cup of wine for Elijah was established by the Talmudists, and the practice of opening the door for the prophet at the seder arose later.

HAGGADAH. The guidebook for conducting the seder (Haggadah means telling in Hebrew). There are many versions, but all are essentially the same in that they tell the story of the exodus. Parts of the Haggadah date back to the days of the Second Temple, while others were added gradually. Until the Middle Ages much of the text was included in the prayer book (siddur), instead of as a separate book.

KIDDUSH CUP. Some families have a cup used only on Passover.

CANDLES. Two are required.

WATER PITCHER, BASIN, AND TOWEL. For the leader's ritual washing of hands.

ARMCHAIR WITH PILLOW. So that the leader of the ceremony can recline, as free people did in the ancient world when they ate. If possible, pillows should be provided for all the participants.

KIPOTS (Yarmulkes). Should be provided for males who do not bring their own.

MENU

Since dinner is not eaten until after the ceremony, timing can be difficult. A practical solution is to serve dishes that can be prepared in advance and warmed up or cooked quickly.

> *Chopped chicken liver or gefilte fish*
> *Chicken soup with matzo balls*
> *Broiled (butterflied) leg of lamb or brisket of beef*
> *Sweet carrots or leek patties*
> *Roasted or mashed potatoes*
> *Tossed green salad*
> *Fruit salad with chocolate sponge cake*
> *Tea and coffee*

TABLE DECORATION

For the seder we usually set the table with our very best linens, dishes, glasses, and silverware. In fact, some families have a special set of dishes that they use only during Passover. The centerpiece of the table is composed mainly of the ceremonial objects. But a variety of decorative elements can be added to enliven the table.

PLACEMENT OF CEREMONIAL OBJECTS

SEDER PLATE.   Center of table.

MATZOS.   If not on seder plate, next to it toward the leader of the ceremony or in front of the leader.

ELIJAH'S CUP.   Next to the seder plate opposite the matzos, if separate from the seder plate, or toward the leader.

CANDLES.   Anywhere, but preferably along the axis of the seder plate, matzos, and Elijah's cup.

HAGGADAH(S).   On the leader's right hand. In addition, if everyone participates in the recitation, one at each plate or – when there aren't enough for everyone – between the place settings.

KIDDUSH CUP.   In front of the leader.

WATER PITCHER, BASIN, AND TOWEL.   To the left of the leader.

INDIVIDUAL SEDER PLATES AND SMALL BOWL OF SALTWATER.   At each place setting.

WINE GLASSES.   One to the right above the knife for every participant, including children even though theirs might be filled with grape juice.

DECORATIVE ELEMENTS

Further decoration of the table is, of course, optional. One advantage is that it provides an opportunity to personalize the table. Following are some suggestions.

LINENS.   White and blue or purple are the traditional colors and can be mixed – white tablecloth with blue or purple napkins or vice versa. But the spring festival aspect of the celebration might be represented with a floral pattern or seasonal colors like green, yellow, or pink. A modern alternative is to use brightly colored place mats, with a paper or cloth runner down the middle of the table. Or instead of the runner, use a map of Israel or yellow paper cut in the shape of the Sinai desert, perhaps decorated with drawings of tents.

BRICKS.   To remind us of the Israelites' role in Egyptian construction, place two or three bricks on the table. They might be used as trivets for hot dishes or as a base for the seder plate.

PYRAMIDS.   In almost everyone's mind, Egypt is symbolized by the pyramid. Lovely glass ones are available in the stores, and children's block sets often include triangular shapes. Place a few around the table. Triangular candle holders (or vases that can be adapted for use as holders) have a dramatic effect, especially when used on an otherwise traditional table.

CANES. Traditionalist Ashkenazi Jews bring canes to the table, in accordance with Exodus 12:11, "And thus shall you eat it: with your loins girded, your shoes on your feet, and your staff in your hand; and you shall eat in haste – it is the Lord's passover." Miniature canes or shepherds' crooks can be made by wrapping brown paper around pipe cleaners, which are bent into a semi-circle at the top. Put one by everyone's individual seder plate.

CAMELS OR HORSES. Use statuettes as part of the centerpiece or decorative elements to represent desert transportation.

FLOWERS. Depending on the size of the table, surround the seder plate with spring flowers and leaves, or place small vases containing one or two blossoms at everyone's place setting.

CACTUS PLANTS. They represent the desert, of course.

SHELLS. Symbols of the escape across the Red Sea.

DOVES. Use paper doves, symbolizing peace, as coasters for the wine glasses, or spread them around the table.

GIFTS FOR THE HOST

Afikomen holder
Candle holder, especially triangular
Candles
Dove made of glass or ceramics
Elijah's cup
Haggadah
Kiddush cup
Matzo holder, with pockets
Pillow – preferably embroidered
Pyramid made of glass or ceramics
Seder plate
Serving tray
Wine glasses

MEMENTOS FOR GUESTS

For children – miniature baskets containing small dolls,
    representing Moses in the bulrushes
Miniature canes
Paper coasters in shape of doves or tents

Paper napkin rings, with quotations about freedom and peace
    written on them
Small vase of flowers at each place setting (it would be especially
    thoughtful if the flowers were the color of the guest's birthstone)

CHECK LIST OF BASICS

Seder plate, with the following ceremonial foods:
    Maror
    Charoset
    Z'roah (bone)
    Beitzah (hard-boiled egg)
    Karpas (parsley or other vegetable)
Matzo
Salt water
Wine
Armchair
Candles
Elijah's cup
Haggadah(s)
Kiddush cup
Kipots (yarmulkes)
Pillow(s)
Water pitcher, with bowl and towel

SUMMARY OF SUGGESTED ORNAMENTS

Bricks
Cactus plants
Camels
Canes
Doves
Flowers
Horses
Pyramids
Shells

RECISES

CHAROSET
(Traditional)

1 cup apples, grated
1 cup walnuts, chopped
1/2 cup almonds, chopped
1/4 tsp. cinnamon
1 tbsp. sweet red wine, or 1 tbsp. honey, or
*   10 dates finely chopped*

Mix all the ingredients, adding more wine or honey if necessary, until mixture has consistency of mortar or clay.

CHAROSET
(Iraqi)

1 cup almonds, finely chopped
1 cup walnuts, finely chopped
1 cup pine nuts, finely chopped
1 tbsp. powdered sugar
3 tbsp. red wine or orange juice

Mix nuts and sugar, then add wine or juice until mixture has consistency of mortar or clay.

CHOPPED CHICKEN LIVER
(See Chapter 3, Rosh Hashanah.)

GEFILTE FISH
(See Chapter 2, Sabbath.)

CHICKEN SOUP
(See Chapter 2, Sabbath.)

MATZO BALLS

For 12 medium-size balls

3 eggs
3/4 cup matzo meal
3 tbsp. water
2 tbsp. vegetable oil
1 tsp. salt
4 quarts chicken broth (can be canned
        or made from cubes)

Mix eggs, oil, and salt. Then thoroughly blend matzo meal into mixture. Add water, and mix again. Cool in refrigerator for one hour. Bring chicken broth to boil. Wetting hands with cold water, shape mixture into balls the size of cherry tomatoes. (Hands must always be wet, otherwise the mixture will stick to them.) Drop balls into boiling broth. Cook until fluffy but firm (15-20 minutes). Remove balls and serve in chicken soup, or place in covered bowl and refrigerate. If refrigerated, allow balls to come to room temperature before serving in soup.

BROILED (BUTTERFLIED) LAMB

Serves 6

One 5-lb. leg of lamb, boned and butterflied
2 cloves garlic, crushed
Salt and black pepper to taste
Mint jelly (optional)

Have butcher bone lamb and spread it out (butterfly it) so that thickness is fairly even. (Save bone for use as Z'roah.) If lamb has been refrigerated, allow it to come to room temperature. Rub thoroughly with garlic. Salt and pepper to taste. Broil (or barbecue over coals) both sides six inches from flame, about 15 minutes a side. (This can be done while diners are eating their appetizer and soup.) Slice thinly against the grain. Serve with mint jelly.

BRISKET
(Also see Chapter 2, Sabbath.)

Serves 8-10

One 5-lb. brisket of beef
1/2 cup dry red wine
1/2 cup water
2 large onions, sliced
2 medium-size carrots, sliced
6-8 cloves of garlic, chopped
1/4 tsp. paprika
2 tsp. salt
Black pepper to taste
1 tsp. sugar
1/4 lb. (1 stick) margarine, melted

Rub garlic, salt, and pepper into meat and sprinkle with paprika. Put the melted margarine, onions, and carrots on bottom of roasting pan. Place meat on rack over mixture. Broil meat on all sides until brown. Reduce heat to 300 degrees. Pour mixture of wine, water, and sugar over meat, cover, and roast until tender (about 2 to 2 1/2 hours). Can be cooked in advance, refrigerated, and reheated.

SWEET CARROTS

Serves 6

12 medium-size carrots
1 1/2 cup chicken broth
4 tbsp. margarine
3 tbsp. sugar
1/2 tsp. salt
Black pepper to taste

Put all ingredients, except carrots, into saucepan, stir, and bring to boil. Reduce heat, add carrots, and simmer until carrots are tender (about 30 minutes). Make sure that carrots remain submerged in liquid while cooking. Remove carrots and continue to simmer liquid until it thickens. Pour liquid over carrots and serve. Can be made in advance, refrigerated, and reheated with carrots in liquid.

ROASTED POTATOES

2 medium-size or 1 large new (white) potatoes per person
Margarine or vegetable oil, melted (enough to coat potatoes
*   and bottom of pan or casserole)*
Salt
Black pepper
Paprika
Parsley, chopped

Be sure to select potatoes that are approximately the same size. Wash potatoes thoroughly, but do not peel. Parboil in salted water until barely tender (about 10 minutes for medium-size potatoes, 15 for large ones). Do not overcook. Pour off water and cover potatoes with cold water. Slip skins off under cold water, and with point of paring knife dig out any dark spots. Drain potatoes, cut medium-size ones in half or large ones into quarters. Coat with melted margarine or oil. Salt each piece to taste and pepper generously. Sprinkle with paprika. Coat bottom of roasting pan or casserole with margarine or oil so potatoes won't stick. Preheat oven to 375 degrees. Roast until tender and brown, turning occasionally and recoating with margarine or oil. (If not brown when tender, broil for a few minutes.) Sprinkle with chopped parsley before serving. May be cooked in advance, refrigerated, and reheated in oven or microwave.

SEPHARDIC LEEK PATTIES

Serves 8 or more

12 very large leeks
3 matzos
3 large eggs
1 tsp. salt
1/4 tsp. black pepper
Matzo meal for dredging
Vegetable oil for frying
Juice of 1 lemon

Cut roots and green leaves off leeks, saving only the white and yellow parts. Cut into small pieces and rinse well to remove sand. Boil in water until soft (about 35 minutes). Meanwhile, soak matzos in warm water until soft. Squeeze water out of leeks and matzos. Chop leeks into coarse pieces. Beat eggs, salt, and pepper into matzos, then beat in leeks. Mixture should be soft and sticky enough to form into patties. If it is too liquid, beat in matzo meal until right consistency. If too dry, add egg. Form small, thick patties and dredge in matzo meal. Preheat oil and fry patties until golden brown on both sides (about 10 minutes). Drain and place in baking dish. Refrigerate overnight or up to three days. To serve, sprinkle liberally with lemon juice and reheat in oven.

CHOCOLATE SPONGE CAKE

Serves 8

1 cup chopped walnuts, pecans, or both
4 tbsp. matzo meal
1 cup semi-sweet chocolate morsels
6 eggs
1 cup sugar

Preheat oven to 350 degrees. Mix nuts, matzo meal, and chocolate, and set aside. Separate whites and yolks of eggs, and put yolks aside. Beat whites with sugar until very stiff. Fold in unbeaten yolks one by one. Then fold in the mixture. Place in cake pan. Bake cake until brown or toothpick inserted in middle comes out clean. Leave in open oven until cool, so it won't fall. Serve with fruit salad.

CHAPTER 9

Yom Ha'Atzmaut: Israeli Independence Day
(Iyar 5: April or May)

Behold, I have set the land before you: go in and possess the land which the Lord swore unto your fathers, to Abraham, to Isaac, and to Jacob, to give to them and to their seed after them. . . .

For the Lord thy God brings you into a good land, a land of brooks and fountains, of springs welling up in valleys and hills; a land of wheat and barley, and vines and fig trees, and pomegranates; a land of olive trees and honey; a land where you will eat bread without scarceness, where you will lack nothing; a land where the stones are iron, and out of whose hills you may dig brass. And you will eat and be satisfied, and bless the Lord your God for the good land He has given you.

Deuteronomy 1:8, 8:7-10

At 4:00 on the afternoon of May 14, 1948, a short, stocky man with a weather-beaten face stepped up to a microphone in the Tel Aviv Museum and read a document that would change the course of Jewish history. "The Land of Israel was the birthplace of the Jewish people," David Ben-Gurion began. "Here their spiritual, religious, and national identity was formed. Here they achieved independence and created a culture of national and universal significance. Here they wrote and gave the Bible to the world.

"Exiled from the Land of Israel, the Jewish people remained faithful to it in all the countries of their dispersion, never ceasing to pray and hope for their return and the restoration of their national freedom.

"Impelled by this historic association, Jews strove throughout the cednturies to go back to the land of their fathers and regain their statehood. In recent decades they returned in their masses. They reclaimed the wilderness, revived their language, built cities and villages, and established a vigorous and ever-growing community, with its own economic and cultural life. They sought peace, yet were prepared to defend themselves. They brought the blessings of progress to all inhabitants of the country and looked forward to sovereign independence."

He went on to summarize the legal and moral foundation for the right of the Jewish people to a national revival in their own country: the Balfour Declaration of 1917, which acknowledged the right of the Jewish people to a National Home; the reaffirmation of the right by the League of Nations when it awarded Great Britain a mandate for the establishment of a government in Palestine; the holocaust which "proved anew the need to solve the problem of the homelessness and lack of independence of the Jewish people by means of the reestablishment of the Jewish State;" and the resolution of the United Nations General Assembly authorizing a Jewish State in Palestine.

"Accordingly," Ben-Gurion continued, "we, the members of the National Council representing the Jewish people in Palestine and World Zionist Movement, are met together in solemn assembly today, the day of termination of the British Mandate for Palestine; and by virtue of the natural and historic right of the Jewish people and of the Resolution of the General Assembly of the United Nations,

"We hereby proclaim the establishment of the Jewish State in Palestine, to be called Medinath Yisrael (The State of Israel). . . .

"The State of Israel will be open to the immigration of Jews from all countries of their dispersion; will promote the development of the country for the benefit of all its inhabitants; will be based on the principles of liberty, justice, and peace as conceived by the Prophets of Israel; will uphold the full social and political equality of all its citizens, without distinction of religion, race, or sex; will guarantee freedom of religion, conscience, education, and culture; will safeguard the Holy Places of all religions; and will loyally uphold the principles of the United Nations Charter. . . .

"With trust in the Rock of Israel, we set our hand to this Declaration, at this session of the Provisional State Council, on the soil of the Homeland, in the city of Tel Aviv, on this Sabbath eve, the fifth of Iyar, 5708, the fourteenth of May, 1948."

The next day the armed forces of neighboring Arab states attacked the new state.

Yom Ha'Atzmaut (Independence Day) celebrations are tempered by the memory of those who died in the War of Independence and subsequent wars. During the morning of Iyar 4 sirens are sounded throughout Israel and all Jews, wherever they are, stop what they are doing and observe a moment of silence. Memorial services are held during the day. When the stars come out that evening, the sirens are sounded again to announce that the period of mourning is over—and the Yom Ha'Atzmaut festivities commence.

After services in the synagogue, families and friends get together for a celebratory meal. At special services the following morning, psalms of thanksgiving are recited and a special memorial prayer is chanted for those who fell in the War of Independence. The rest of the day is devoted to parades, especially in the large cities. Many families end the day with picnics.

YOM HA'ATZMAUT SYMBOLS

The holiday is represented, of course, by the flag, seal, and national anthem of Israel.

FLAG. The Israeli flag is white with two light-blue stripes and a blue Star of David in the middle. Hence representative colors for the holiday are white and blue. The flag was unfurled for the first time at Lake Success in New York State on May 11, 1949, when Israel became the fifty-ninth member of the United Nations.

SEAL. The seal of the State of Israel—its national emblem—is a white seven-branched menorah with a white olive branch on each side on a blue background. It is derived from a seal taken from the Second Temple by the Romans.

NATIONAL ANTHEM. Israel's national anthem is the "Hatikva." The words were written in 1878 by Naphtali Hertz Imber. After he read it to the early agricultural settlement of Rishon Le-Zyyon in 1882, one of the settlers, Samuel Cohen, set it to music. The song became the anthem of the Yishuv (Jewish Settlement in Palestine).

TRADITIONAL FOODS

Typical Israeli foods are usually served on the holiday, particularly falafel (a grain and vegetable mixture made into hamburger-like patties) inserted into the pocket of a pita bread. Other regional foods include taboula (a kind of salad made of bulgur wheat and vegetables), hummous (a bean dish), dolmas (meat-stuffed vegetable), skewered lamb or beef, baklava, and salads composed of local produce.

MENU

The following menu is for an elaborate buffet and therefore includes a broad range of dishes. For a smaller gathering select a dish from each category.

Appetizer (served with pita)
Hummus
Tahini
Main Course
Falafel
Middle Eastern chicken
Kebab
Shashlik
Dolmas
Couscous with meat and vegetables
Vegetable
Eggplant
Rice with pine nuts
Taboula
Salad
Gourmet-pepper salad
Israeli salad
Dessert
Baklava
Fresh Fruit

TABLE DECORATION

Like the Fourth of July in the United States and independence days in many other countries, Yom Ha'Atzmaut is party time. If you're inviting a lot of people over to celebrate with you, the most practical way to serve dinner is a buffet. But the occasion certainly also merits a formal dinner. For your table decoration, the colors of the day are blue and white and the ornaments should be symbols of Israel, including those expressing the wish for peace:

LINENS.

- A blue tablecloth with white napkins, or vice versa, would establish the patriotic theme. You might encircle the napkins with olive branches, if you can obtain some. Otherwise tie contrasting blue or white ribbons around the napkins, and insert small Israeli flags between the riboons and the napkins.

- As a tablecloth, use a map of Israel. Around white napkins, tie blue ribbons.

- If you're dining at the table, you might lay blue place mats on a white tablecloth. Use blue napkins.

- On a paper tablecloth, paste Israeli stamps (you can buy inexpensive sets at stamp stores).

- Symbolize Israel's reclamation of the desert with a yellow tablecloth, brown napkins, and a centerpiece consisting of colorful flowers.

CENTERPIECE.

- A seven-branch menorah represents the holiday perfectly. Surround it with olive branches, if you can.

- Fill a vase with blue and white flowers, and surround it with small Israeli flags.

- In small vases lined up in the center of the table, put blue and white flowers and Israeli flags. Between the vases and at the ends of the line place small white and blue candles.

- Cluster Israeli flags on a map of the country.

- Arrange bright flowers around a cactus plant to represent the reclamation of the desert.

ORNAMENTS.

- Ceramic, plastic, or paper doves.

- Stars of David.

- Miniature seven-branched menorahs.

- Figurines or dolls dressed in costumes worn by the various ethnic groups comprising the population of Israel. (They are sold in Jewish gift shops. If you have a collection, group them around an Israeli flag as a centerpiece.)

- Israeli flags.
- Candles in many colors, symbolizing the people of different religions and nationalities who live in Israel.
- Blue and white ribbons, tied around the stems of wine glasses.

GIFTS FOR THE HOST

Book about Israel
Israeli wine
Figurine or doll dressed in ethnic costume
Plaque or photograph showing the bronze menorah that
      stands in front of the Knesset in Israel (obtainable in many
      Jewish gift shops and book stores)
Recording of Israeli music
Seven-branched menorah

MEMENTOS FOR GUESTS

Blue and white flowers
Dove (paper or plastic)
Israeli flag
Menorah (miniature)
Olive branch

SUMMARY OF SUGGESTED ORNAMENTS

Cactus plant
Candles, blue and white, or many different colors
Doves
Figurines or dolls representing ethnic groups
Flowers, blue and white
Israeli flags
Menorahs (miniature)
Olive branches
Ribbons, blue and white
Stars of David

RECIPES

HUMMUS

Serves 10

2 cans garbanzo beans
1/2 cup tahini (from can or jar)
1/2 cup water
3 cloves garlic, minced
1/8 tsp. cumin
Juice of 1/2 lemon
Salt and pepper to taste

Mix ingredients in food processor or blender until smooth. Decorate mixture with paprika and sprinkle with a little olive oil. Serve in bowl lined with lettuce, accompanied by pita.

TAHINI

Serves 4-6

1 cup tahini (from can or jar)
1 cup water
Juice of 1/2 lemon

Mix ingredients in food processor or blender until smooth. Decorate with parsley, and serve with pita.

FALAFEL

50-60 Patties

1/3 cup cracked wheat
1/2 lb. garbanzo beans (chick peas)
2 slices of dry bread
5 garlic cloves, minced
2 tbsp. parsley, chopped
3 tbsp. lemon juice
1 tsp. cumin
1/4 tsp. coriander
Salt and pepper to taste
Hot red pepper, dash (optional)
2 eggs
1/2 cup bread crumbs, unseasoned
Oil, vegetable or olive

Soak beans overnight in enough water to cover. When ready to prepare, drain and rinse beans. Put in a large pot, cover with fresh water, add one teaspoon salt and bring to a boil.

Reduce heat and simmer for 1 1/2 to 2 hours. Remove from heat and drain. While beans are cooking, soak cracked wheat in a bowl for about 10 minutes. In another small bowl, soak the slices of dry bread. Grind the garbanzo beans in a food processor with garlic and parsley. Squeeze water out of bread and add to bean mixture. Add remaining salt, lemon juice, seasonings, and eggs. Mix lightly. Drain the cracked wheat and add to the mixture with half of the bread crumbs. Stir thoroughly while adding the rest of the bread crumbs. Shape mixture into small patties or balls, approximately one inch in diameter. adding more crumbs if needed. Put 1 to 1 1/2 in. oil in heavy frying pan and heat to approximately 375 degrees. Drop falafel balls into the hot fat, a few at a time and cook until deep golden brown. Remove from heat when cooked and drain on paper towels. The mixture may be prepared a day or so in advance, and cooked when desired. Serve on a large platter and garnish with parsley and thin lemon slices.

MIDDLE EASTERN CHICKEN

Serves 4-6

1 chicken, cut into eight pieces
2 cloves garlic, diced
2 cups tomatoes, chopped
2 large yellow onions, chopped
1 large green pepper
4 tbsp. pine nuts
1 cup water
1/2 cup olive oil
Salt and pepper to taste

Preheat oven to 300 degrees. Brown chicken in oil and place in roaster. Add other ingredients, including oil that remains after browning. Cover and bake for one hour or until chicken is tender and well-cooked.

KEBAB

Serves 4-6

2 lbs. beef or lamb, chopped
2 eggs
1/4 cup bread crumbs
1 bunch cilantro, chopped
Salt, pepper, and cumin to taste
Onions, green peppers, and/or cherry tomatoes

Mix meat, eggs, bread crumbs, cilantro, and seasoning, and form into spoon-size balls. Skewer balls and vegetables, two balls per skewer with slices of onion, chunks of green pepper, and/or cherry tomatoes in between. Broil for 10 minutes or until brown, or barbeque.

SHASHLIK

Similar to kebab, above, but with meat cut into cubes instead of mixed with other ingredients to form balls. Put three or more cubes on each skewer, separated by vegetables, and broil or barbeque. Plan for one or two skewers per person.

DOLMAS
(See Chapter 7, Purim.)

COUSCOUS
(See Chapter 7, Purim.)

EGGPLANT
(Vegetable or Dip)

Serves 6-8

2 eggplants, about 1 lb. each
3 tbsp. mayonnaise or tahini
Juice of 1 lemon
Salt, pepper, and garlic powder to taste

Slash skins of eggplants in several places, cover with aluminum foil, and broil or barbeque for 1/2 hour. When cool, cut each eggplant in half, scoop out flesh, and mix thoroughly with other ingredients. Place in bowl and decorate with chopped parsley. Serve as dip or as side dish on lettuce leaves.

RICE WITH ALMONDS
(see Chapter 6, Tu Be Shevat.)

TABOULA

Serves 4-6

1/2 cup bulgur
8-10 spring onions (scallions)
1 1/2 tsp. black pepper
5 cups parsley, chopped
3 medium tomatoes, chopped fine
1 tsp. cilantro, chopped
1/4 cup lemon juice
1/4 cup olive oil

Rinse bulgur, drain well, place in bowl, and refrigerate for one hour. (If using packaged bulgur, follow directions on package.) Cut onions in small pieces (including green tops), mix with salt, pepper, parsley, and cilantro, and stir into bulgur. Spread tomatoes on top. Just before serving, mix lemon juice with olive oil, pour over salad, and allow to seep in.

GOURMET PEPPER SALAD

Serves 6

2 large green peppers, cut into strips
2 large red sweet peppers, cut into strips
1 lb. mushrooms, sliced
2 tbsp. raisins
3 tbsp. pine nuts, toasted
4 tbsp. sliced almonds, toasted
2 tbsp. olive oil
Juice of 1/2 lemon
2 tbsp. soy sauce
Salt and pepper to taste

Pour olive oil into frying pan, saute peppers and mushrooms for four to five minutes, then add raisins, lemon juice, soy sauce, salt, and pepper. Stir, and remove from heat. Sprinkle pine nuts and almonds across top before serving.

ISRAELI SALAD

Serves 8-12

6 large tomatoes, chopped
3 large cucumbers, chopped
1/4 yellow onion, chopped
10 pitted black olives, chopped
10 pitted green olives, chopped
1/8 tsp. parsley, chopped

Mix ingredients. Add dressing just before serving.

Dressing
2 tbsp. lemon juice
3 tbsp. olive oil
Salt and pepper to taste

Mix ingredients. Shake well before pouring.

BAKLAVA

100-150 pieces

5 cups walnuts, chopped
1 tbsp. ground cinnamon
1/2 tsp. nutmeg
1/4 tsp. cloves
1/2 cup sugar
2 boxes filo dough (discard any dry, crumbled,
   or cracked pastry skins)
2 cups sweet butter, melted

Preheat oven to 350 degrees. Mix nuts, cinnamon, nutmeg, cloves, and sugar. In buttered pan, stack 12 filo sheets, brushing each with butter. Spread one cup nut mixture on top. Repeat, but with fewer sheets (8–10). Build enough layers to use all the nut mixture, then add the remaining sheets of dough. Brush extra butter on top. Place in oven and immediately reduce heat to 200 degrees. Bake for 30 minutes.

CHAPTER 10

Lag Ba'Omer
(Iyar 18: April or May)

And you shall count from the day after the day of rest, from the day you brought the sheaf of wave offering, seven complete weeks.

Leviticus 23:15

Starting the second day of Passover, there is a seven-week period of mourning, the omer, which ends the day before Shavuoth. Traditionally, marriages, celebrations, parties, hair cuts, and other practices are forbidden during the omer—except on one day, Lag Ba'Omer. The name means thirty-third day of the omer. In the word Lag, the first two letters transliterate the Hebrew letter lamedh, which represents the number 30, and the g is gimel or 3. Omer in ancient Hebrew was a unit of dry measure equal to about one-half peck. On the day after Passover Israelite farmers were obliged to make an offering of an omer of barley.

While the Torah specifically requires the barley offering and the celebration of Shavuoth after the lapse of seven weeks, it says nothing about a period of mourning or about Lag Ba'Omer. Nor is it known when and why either was introduced. One theory is that the mourning memorializes the Jews who were killed in the rebellion against the Romans led by Simeon bar Kosiba in 132-5. The uprising, known as the Second Judean Revolt or Second Roman War, was precipitated by the Emperor Hadrian's decree restructuring Jerusalem as a Roman colony. Lag Ba'Omer might be a celebration of Simeon's short-lived occupation of Jerusalem. After the defeat of the rebellion, Hadrian changed the name of Judea to Syria Palestina and prohibited Jews from entering Jerusalem, which he renamed Aelia Capitolina.

Another interpretation, based on a passage in the Talmud, is that the mourning is for Rabbi Akiba ben Joseph's disciples who died in a plague because they lacked proper respect for each other. Lag Ba'Omer commemorates a day's respite from the pestilence or the day it ended.[1] However, the memorial for the disciples might have another foundation related to the Rabbi and his followers. Although an illiterate shepherd, Akiba married the daughter of one of Jerusalem's wealthiest men, who was furious at the match and refused to support them, with the result that they lived in dire poverty. Akiba learned to read when he was forty, and with his wife's encouragement went away to study under leading scholars of the time. His erudition and original insights into the Torah won him a large following of disciples. When the Second Judean Revolt broke out, he put his disciples at the disposal

---

[1] Michael Strassfeld, *The Jewish Holidays: A Guide and Commentary* (New York: Harper & Row Publishers, 1985), p. 50.

111

of Simeon bar Kosiba, and most of them were killed in the war. After the war, the Romans outlawed the study of the Torah as part of their effort to crush the Jews. But Akiba continued to teach, gathering around him a new group of scholars. The Romans arrested him and tortured him to death.[2]

Among Akiba's latter group of disciples was Rabbi Simeon bar Yohai. Like his master, Simeon refused to stop teaching the Torah and was forced to hide in a cave on Mount Meron for twelve years, surviving mainly on carob and fruit that grew wild nearby. Students who visited the cave to study under Simeon's tutelage carried bows and arrows to deceive the Romans by appearing like hunters. Presumably, they carried the subterfuge further by actually hunting and eating their kill. Simeon bar Yohai is said to have died on Lag Ba'Omer, and a great fire was seen burning at the cave.

From this story arose the custom of having picnics on Lag Ba'Omer and shooting arrows. In Israel people visit the rabbi's tomb on Mount Meron and in the evening light a bonfire, which they keep burning until midnight. A tradition developed in the sixteenth century, and still practiced by some Jewish families, is have a rabbi give three-year-old boys their first haircuts at the celebration on Mount Meron. The shorn locks are thrown into the bonfire to bring good luck.

Since weddings are not allowed during the omer, except on Lag Ba'Omer, more marriages are performed on that day in Israel than at any other time during the year. There also are a lot of parties, and amateur sports are popular. That is to say, Lag Ba'Omer is a happy day, a relief from the gloom of the omer. Bright colors reflect the joyful spirit of the holiday—red, orange, yellow.

MENU

Even if a picnic is impractical because of wet or chilly spring weather, picnic-type foods (with a Jewish touch, of course) are definitely in order. In Israel carob and other fruit are usually included in commemoration of Simeon bar Yohai's diet. The menu might include:

> *Relish tray containing olives, pickles, radishes, scallions, celery*
> *Hamburgers and/or hot dogs*
> *Chopped eggplant, marinated broccoli, and/or*
> *baked mixed vegetables,*
> *Spiced potatoes or potato kugel*
> *Carob and other fruit*
> *Lemon bars*
> *Sesame treats*

TABLE DECORATION

Whether you go on a picnic or eat at home, you'll probably want to set a buffet table because it's suitable for a picnic-type meal. But the decoration for a regular dinner would

---

2 Adin Steinsaltz, *The Essential Talmud,* trans. by Chaya Galai (London: Weidenfeld and Nicolson, 1976), pp. 29-30. However, some scholars question the tradition about Akiba's support of the rebellion.

be about the same. If you have a quiver full of arrows (real ones or toys) it would be an ideal centerpiece, or if you just have the arrows put them in a vase. Otherwise use a dart game to represent a bow and arrows. Ornaments might include:

- Figurines of a shepherd and a lamb (depicting Rabbi Akiba ben Joseph).

- A bicycle, for the sports aspect of the holiday.

- Wheat (the omer).

- A hand-shaped amulet for good luck.

- Wedding rings, especially the large Jewish ceremonial ones that once were used in European communities.

- Carob, which Rabbi Simeon bar Yohai is said to have lived on while hiding in a cave.

Another approach is to focus on a theme associated with Lag Ba'Omer (however, the decorations are interchangeable if you want to combine ideas):

WEDDING TABLE. Whether or not your guests know that Lag Ba'Omer is a favorite day for marriages, a wedding theme would establish a merry atmosphere for the meal. If they don't know, part of the fun will be their surprise. On a red tablecloth group small candles in glass holders around a bridal tiara cut out of white or gold cardboard as a centerpiece. (Attach a piece of cheesecloth as a veil.) An alternative centerpiece can be created by wrapping a tiara around a bouquet of flowers. Or if you have bride and groom figurines or dolls, use them and stretch a huppah over their heads. (An easy way to make a huppah is to cut out pieces from the four sides of an open cardboard box so that the four corners remain, and paste a piece of cloth over the closed end.) Use gold ribbons or strips of gold paper, pasted at the ends, as napkin rings—representing wedding rings. The napkins should be white or blue to contrast with the red tablecloth. Place a wedding invitation on every napkin—but without the names of the bride and groom. Invite your guests to fill in the names. They're bound to know a couple they'd like to see married. Flowers, either strewn around the table or put in small vases, would be the ornaments.

RABBI AKIBA TABLE. For your linens use the blue and white traditional Jewish colors. A toy sheep or figurines of a shepherd and sheep would constitute the centerpiece. Ornaments might include a book—especially a Torah—representing the Rabbi's erudition; wheat, for the omer; and olive branches, symbolizing peace in memory of his slain disciples; and perhaps a figurine of a fox. The fox refers to a parable told by Rabbi Akiba when a friend warned him about the dangers of continuing to teach the Torah. "The fox saw the fish fleeing the nets in the water and proposed to them that they come and live on dry land. They said to him: 'Fox, you are not the wisest of animals, but a fool. If we live in fear in the water which is our habitat, how much more will we fear on dry land, where we will find our death.' "[3]

SIMEON BAR KOSIBA TABLE. Memorialize the disastrous Second Judean Revolt by emphasizing peace. Base your decoration on Isaiah's vision of the day when the nations

---

[3] Quote by Steinsaltz, *ibid,* p. 30.

will "beat their swords into plowshares, and their spears into pruning hooks: nation will not lift up sword against nation, nor will they learn war any more." (Isaiah 2:4). Represent agriculture with a brown tablecloth and green napkins, or vice versa, and create a centerpiece by grouping miniature farming tools, swords, and spears. To make the point clear, put a sign next to the centerpiece quoting Isaiah.

SPORTS TABLE. On a green or brown tablecloth (the playing field), place a football, basketball, soccerball, volleyball, figurine of a horse (if you're interest is in riding or other equestrian sport), set of miniature golf clubs, or whatever as a centerpiece, depending on your favorite sport. You might even use a tennis shoe, with some flowers in it. But also put some more direct symbols of the holiday on the table, like wheat, carob, miniature bows and arrows, or figurines of a lamb and shepherd.

GIFTS FOR THE HOST

Amulet for good luck
Apron
Book about Lag Ba'Omer
Bow and arrows
Carob candy
Figurine of shepherd, lamb, fox
Flowers
Log for bonfire or fireplace
Measuring cup (for wheat—perhaps with flour in it)
Paper napkins
Skewers for barbecue
Sport's object

MEMENTOS FOR GUESTS

Bow and arrows (miniature toys)
Carob
Game (miniature)
Lamb (paper)
Matches
Ring (paper or plastic, of course)
Wedding invitation (without names)

SUMMARY OF SUGGESTED ORNAMENTS

Amulet
Arrows
Bicycle (miniature)
Book
Bouquet
Bow (and arrows)

Bridal tiara
Bride & groom figurines
Candles
Carob
Darts
Farming tools
Flowers
Fox
Game
Huppah
Isaiah quotation
Lamb or sheep figurine
Olive branches
Ring
Shepherd figurine
Spears (miniature)
Sport's object
Swords (miniature)
Tennis shoe
Torah (miniature)
Wedding invitations
Wheat

RECIPES

HAMBURGERS

Serves 6-8

2 lbs. ground meat
2 eggs
2 onions, chopped
2 carrots, grated
1 tsp. salt
1/2 tsp. black pepper
3 tbsp. cracker meal
3 tbsp. wheat germ (6 tbsp. if
    cracker meal is not available)

Combine ingredients and mix well. Form into patties. Fry on both sides until done or place on grill and barbecue.

CHOPPED EGGPLANT

Serves 6-8

2 lbs. eggplant
1/2 to 3/4 cup flour
1 large onion, chopped
1/8 tsp. garlic
Oil for frying
2 hard-boiled eggs
Salt and pepper to taste

Wash eggplant, peel, and slice into 1/2-in.-thick pieces. Sprinkle with salt and let stand until bitterness is drawn out. Wash slices under running water, dry with paper towels, and sprinkle with flour. Heat oil in a large skillet. Fry eggplant until brown on both sides, remove from skillet, and blot excess oil. Mix together onion and garlic powder and fry in remaining oil until golden brown. Mix eggplant, onion, and eggs in a food processor until smooth. Add salt and pepper and place in refrigerator to chill. Before serving, garnish with parsley, lemon wedges, olives, and chopped walnuts.

MARINATED BROCCOLI

Serves 6-8

2 bunches broccoli
1 tsp. ginger powder
2 tbsp. olive oil
3 tbsp. sherry
3 tbsp. water
2 tsp. sugar
1/4 tsp. salt

Separate broccoli florets from stems and slice stems diagonally. Combine other ingredients and mix well. Pour mixture over broccoli, cover, and place in refrigerator for six hours, turning the broccoli over from time to time. Before serving, saute broccoli in the marinade for five minutes. Turn broccoli over a few times while sauteing.

SPICED POTATOES

Serves 6-8

8 medium or large potatoes, peeled
(Cover with water until ready to use.)
1/2 cup olive oil
1 tsp. paprika
1/8 tsp. garlic powder
1/2 tsp. onion powder
1/4 tsp. salt

Preheat oven to 350 degrees. Mix olive oil, spices, and salt. Dry potatoes, cut into halves, place in baking pan, and brush with oil-spice mixture. Bake uncovered for one hour or until soft and browned.

POTATO KUGEL

Serves 6-8

3 onions, minced
4 zucchinis, grated
5 carrots, grated
1 large potato, grated
5 eggs
3/4 cup matzo meal or 1 cup flour
1 tsp. baking powder
1/8 tsp. paprika
1 tsp. salt
1/4 tsp. pepper

Preheat oven to 375 degrees. Mix baking powder with matzo meal or flour, add remaining ingredients, and mix thoroughly by hand. Place mixture in greased 13x9-in. baking pan and bake for one hour. Kugel should be nicely browned and crisp on top.

LAYERED BAKED VEGETABLES

Serves 6-8

1 eggplant, sliced
2 large zucchinis, sliced
1/4 lb. mushrooms, sliced
1 green pepper, cut and separated into rings
1 large onion, cut into rings
2 large tomatoes, sliced
1/2 tsp. salt
1/2 tsp. fresh garlic, minced
3/4 cup olive oil
1/2 tsp. oregano
1/4 tsp. dill

Preheat oven to 350 degrees. Thoroughly mix together salt, garlic, olive oil, and oregano. Cover bottom of greased pan with 1/2-in.-thick zucchini slices and sprinkle with part of oil-spice mixture. Add layer of eggplant slices and again sprinkle with mixture. Put pepper rings and onion rings on top and pour rest of mixture over them. Cover, and bake for 45 minutes. Add tomato and mushroom slices and sprinkle with dill. Bake, uncovered, for additional 10 minutes.

LEMON BARS

Serves 4-6

Dough
1 cup flour
1/4 cup powdered sugar
1/2 cup margarine, melted

Preheat oven to 350 degrees. Mix ingredients to form dough, then pat into 8-in.-square baking pan. Bake for 20 minutes, then allow to cool.

Topping
1 cup sugar
2 tbsp. flour
1/2 tsp. baking powder
3-4 tbsp. lemon juice
2 eggs

Combine ingredients and mix until smooth. Pour over baked dough, spread evenly, and bake at 350 degrees for an additional 25 minutes. Allow to cool, then cut into squares.

SESAME TREATS

Serves 4-6

1 1/2 cup sesame seeds
2 tbsp. oil
3 tbsp. flour
3 tbsp. sugar
1 tbsp. lemon juice

Preheat oven to 400 degrees. Combine ingredients and mix well to make firm dough. If necessary, add a little water to hold dough together. Form into cookies, place on greased baking sheet, and bake for 15 minutes. Allow to cool.

CHAPTER 11

Shavuoth
(Sivan 6–7: May or June)

*You shall count seven weeks; begin to count the seven weeks from the time
you begin to put the sickle to the standing grain. And you shall keep the
feast of weeks for the Lord your God with a free-will offering from your
hand, which you shall give to the Lord your God in proportion to how the
Lord your God has blessed you; and you shall rejoice before the Lord your
God, you and your son, and your daughter, and your man-servant, and your
maid-servant, and the Levite who is within your gates, and the stranger, and
the fatherless, and the widow, who are among you, in the place where the
Lord your God chooses to cause His name to dwell.*

Deuteronomy 16:9-11

Shavuoth is the Hebrew word for weeks, and the name of the holiday comes from the Torah's instructions to celebrate a feast seven weeks after the beginning of the grain harvest. The count starts on the first day of the omer (the second day of Passover), when farmers in the Holy Land used to take a measure (omer) of their barley crop to the Temple as an offering. By the time seven weeks had elapsed, the grain harvest had been completed with the cutting of the wheat. Shavuoth, therefore, was intended as a harvest festival, and indeed the Torah also refers to it as the feast of harvest (hag ha-kazir). On the holiday farmers made other offerings at the Temple, in accordance with the Torah's enjoinder to sacrifice the first fruits of a harvest. They would take two loaves of bread baked from the newly harvested wheat, the first produce in each crop, and even the first animal born in every species raised for food. Hence Shavuoth is also called the day of the first fruits (yom ha-bikurum).

After the destruction of the Second Temple, the feast acquired an additional, immensely profound significance. It became a celebration of the revelation of the Ten Commandments, and thus the Torah, on Mount Sinai. Exactly how, why, or when the change occurred is unknown. Nowhere does the Bible associate Shavuoth with the anniversary of the revelation. However, in Exodus it does say that the Israelites entered the wilderness and encamped before Mount Sinai "in the third month after the children of Israel left the land of Egypt" – that is, in the month of Sivan. Shavuoth thus became the third pilgrimage festival, along with Passover and Sukkoth.

Sometime later the custom developed in Eastern Europe of reading the Book of Ruth in the synagogue on Shavuoth. Set in the era of the Judges, the book tells the story of the close friendship of Naomi and her daughter-in-law Ruth. To escape a famine in Bethlehem, a man named Elimelech took his wife Naomi and their two sons to Moab, a land to the east of the Dead Sea and Jordan River. Elimelech died, but his family stayed in Moab and his sons married Moabite women, Orpah and Ruth. Then the sons also died, and Naomi and her daughters-in-law decided to return to Judeah. On the way, however, Naomi urged Orpah and Ruth to go back to their mothers' homes. Orpah did so, but Ruth stayed. Naomi again urged Ruth to return to her home. Ruth replied: "Wherever you go, I will go. Wherever you live, I will live. Your people shall be my people, and your God my God. Wherever you die, I will die, and there will I be buried. Let the Lord do that to me and even more if anything but death parts you and me."

They arrived in Bethlehem during the Barley harvest, and Ruth offered to go into the fields to pick up grain dropped by the harvesters. (The poor had this right.) She happened to come to a field that belonged to a kinsman of Naomi's husband, a prosperous farmer named Boaz. After enquiring about Ruth and learning of her loyalty to Naomi, Boaz insisted that she stay in his field and ordered the young men not to disturb her. He invited her to have lunch with him, after which he quietly gave instructions to the harvesters to let some grain fall out of their bundles for Ruth. She continued thereafter to go to Boaz's field every day until the harvest was over.

Then Naomi said to her, "Is it not my duty to see that you're well taken care of?" She told Ruth to dress in her best clothes and go that night to visit Boaz, who would be at the threshing floor winnowing the barley. "Do not let him see you before he has finished eating and drinking. When he settles down to sleep, take note of where he lies, slip into the threshing floor, uncover his feet, and lie there. He will tell you what to do." Ruth did as she was instructed. When Boaz awoke and found her, she asked him to "spread your skirt over your handmaiden"—that is, to marry her. In doing so and producing children by Ruth, he would be perpetuating through her Elimelech's name. They married, and Ruth had a son named Obed, who became the father of Jesse, who in turn became the father of David. Tradition has it that David was born on Shavuoth.

In some congregations confirmation ceremonies for students, marking their completion of Hebrew school, are held on Shavuoth. The custom is reminiscent of the medieval practice of starting a child's Torah education on that day. To make the experience as pleasant as possible, the teacher would give the child a tablet with the Hebrew letters on it and would put a little bit of honey on each letter. As the child learned the letter, he would be permitted to lick the honey.

The spirit of the Shavuoth celebration is thus very complex, combining joyous thanksgiving for the gift of agriculture, profound moral gratitude for the Revelation of the Ten Commandments, loving appreciation for the grace of friendship, and humble acceptance of the knowledge bestowed through study of the Torah. Many colors represent the holiday: all those we find in fruits and vegetables, and purple or deep blue and white for the Torah. The holiday is celebrated for two days in the Diaspora, but only for one in Israel.

TRADITIONAL OBJECTS AND FOODS

Despite the importance of Shavuoth, no specific ritual is prescribed, except for saying kiddush and lighting candles of course. However, a number of customs have developed in regard to the observance. Some traditionalists spend the entire night before Shavuoth in the synagogue reading the Torah and other books of the Bible. In Israel people contribute fruit to the National Fund, and the kibbutzim and other agricultural communities take fruit and vegetables to a central location for distribution to the poor. On the evening of the holiday many people wear new clothes, because the Israelites were required to cleanse themselves before the Revelation of the Ten Commandments. Other customs relate to the observance at home:

GREENERY AND FLOWERS. We decorate the house and the synagogue with greenery of all sorts — plants, branches, even trees — and with flowers, particularly roses. (In Italy and Spain, Shavuoth was called the Holiday of the Roses.) The origin of the custom is unknown, but it is probably rooted in the ancient harvest celebration.

DAIRY PRODUCTS. As on all festivals, a celebratory meal is served. But this time it is customary to eat only dairy products — no meat. According to one interpretation, the reason is that after receiving the Ten Commandments at Mount Sinai the Israelites were too hungry to take the time to prepare a meat dish. Another is that when the Israelites learned the laws of kashrut, they were obliged to eat uncooked dairy foods because their cooking pots had been used for both meat and dairy products.

TWO CHALLAHS. In memory of the offerings brought to the Temple, we put two long loaves of challah on the table.

FRUIT. Recalling the offering of the first fruits, we serve fruit, especially species grown in Israel.

MENU

Challah, two loaves
Pickled salmon or other fish (appetizer)
Buttermilk-cucumber soup
Blintzes, or cheese-noodle casserole, or artichoke kugel
Almond-studded squash, or zucchini cheese puff, or noodle
and spinach casserole, or eggplant caponata
Mushroom salad, or fresh spinach salad
Fruit, or apricot or peach halves with cream cheese
Cheesecake, or graham cracker cheesecake,
or fresh fruit torte, or nut bread, or mondelbrot
Wine

TABLE DECORATION

You can represent the holiday simply but elegantly by using a green tablecloth, the Torah surrounded by leaves as a centerpiece, a bowl of fruit garnished with sprigs of wheat, and flowers. A figurine of a cow and and a bowl of honey symbolize the Bible's description of Israel as the "land of milk and honey." A camel signifies the desert, where the Israelites received the Ten Commandments. Possible alternatives include:

LINENS.

- Emphasize the harvest aspect of the holiday by spreading leaves and flowers on a white tablecloth, or by using a floral tablecloth.

- A purple tablecloth with white napkins creates a more somber mood, in keeping with the anniversary of the Revelation.

- Subtly represent both the spiritual and sensuous facets of the celebration by combining a dark blue tablecloth with yellow napkins. Tie a string around the napkins, and insert a stalk of wheat or a flower.

CENTERPIECES.

- Surround a basket of fruit with stalks of wheat. Under the basket place a bed of leaves.

- Create a tableau of the story of Ruth with dolls or figurines representing Naomi, Ruth, and Boaz, a basket full of barley, and a cardboard replica of the Tables of the Law symbolizing the Moabite Ruth's conversion to Judaism.

- Arrange branches and flowers around a cardboard or plastic reproduction of the Second Temple (available in many Jewish gift shops).

- Build a structure out of blocks with Hebrew letters on them, representing the medieval practice of starting a child's Torah education. Surround the structure with branches.

- Fill a vase with roses—different colors, if possible.

- Represent the Torah as the Tree of Life with an artificial tree or, better still, a bonsai, if you have one.

- Use a plant, preferably a flowering one.

- Line up garlands of branches or flowers in the center of the table, and place a serving dish of food in the center of each garland (for family-style meals, where all the dishes are placed on the table instead of being served individually).

ORNAMENTS.

- Scrolls containing the Book of Ruth (miniature).

- Flowers.

- Branches.

- Fruit.

- Cards cut in shape of the Tablets of the Law.

- Plants (small).

- Reeds or straw baskets (a traditional German and Polish decoration on Shavuoth, reminding us of the infant Moses in the ark made of bulrushes).

GIFTS FOR THE HOST

Basket of fruit
Bookends
Book of Ruth inscribed on scroll
Dish for blintzes
Flowers
Honey in jar
Plant
Torah (miniature)
Wine

MEMENTOS FOR GUESTS

Basket (tiny), filled with raisins and olives
Camel (figurine)
Challah (roll size)
Leaf (imitation)
Rose
Tables of the Law (on cardboard or paper)
Wheat stalk

CHECKLIST OF BASICS

Greenery
Flowers
Challah (2 loaves)
Dairy food
Fruit
Candles
Kiddush cup
Kipots (yarmulkes)

SUMMARY OF SUGGESTED ORNAMENTS

Barley in basket
Blocks with Hebrew letters
Boaz (figurine)
Branches
Camel (figurine)
Cow (figurine)
Flowers (especially roses)
Fruit
Honey

Leaves
Naomi (figurine)
Plant(s)
Reeds
Ruth (figurine)
Scroll containing Book of Ruth (miniature)
Straw basket
Tables of the Law (cardboard or paper)
Wheat

RECIPES

PICKLED FISH

Serves 50-60

Two 5-lb. salmon, halibut, or similar fish
1 onion, diced
2 carrots, peeled, sliced at an angle
2 stalks celery, sliced
1 cup white vinegar
2-3 cups sugar
2 tsp. paprika
Juice of 1 lemon
3 bay leaves
1 1/2 tsp. pickling spices

Cook onion, carrots, celery, vinegar, sugar, and paprika for seven minutes in large pot. Wash fish several times inside and out. Remove head and end of tail and cut into 3/4-in. chunks. Place in boiling mixture, reduce heat and cook until fish loses its translucency and turns opaque. Transfer to storage dish, sprinkle with lemon juice and spices, and refrigerate. Keeps for up to one month. Serve as an appetizer.

BUTTERMILK-CUCUMBER SOUP

Serves 4

1 quart buttermilk or yogurt
1 large cucumber, peeled
1 tbsp. olive oil
1 level tsp. dill
1 tbsp. lemon juice
1 clove garlic, mashed
Salt to taste
Green onions, chopped, for garnish

Dice cucumber or cut into thin slices. Mix all ingredients thoroughly and serve, cold, with green onions sprinkled on top.

BLINTZES
(See Chapter 5, Hanukkah.)

CHEESE-NOODLE CASSEROLE

Serves 6-8

1 lb. wide egg noodles
1 cup sour cream
1 cup cottage cheese
1 cube butter or margarine
3 eggs
Salt and pepper to taste

Preheat oven to 450 degrees. Boil noodles until tender and drain. Add the butter and mix until it is melted. Add remaining ingredients, mix well, and pour into greased casserole. Bake for 10 minutes, then lower heat to 300 degrees and bake for additional 1 to 1 1/2 hours.

ARTICHOKE KUGEL

Serves 12-14

1 lb. cheddar cheese, grated
Two 4-oz. jars marinated artichokes
3 bunches green onions, sliced
10 eggs
10 saltine crackers, crumbled
1/2 bunch parsley, chopped
Salt and pepper to taste

Preheat oven to 325 degrees. Drain the liquid from the artichokes and saute the onions in the marinade. Allow to cool. Beat eggs, combine with cracker crumbs, parsley, salt and pepper and mix well. Add cheese, artichokes, and onions and bake for 1 hour in greased 9x13 pan. Cut into pieces and serve either hot or cold.

ALMOND-STUDDED ACORN SQUASH

Serves 4

2 acorn squash
4 tbsp. butter or margarine
1 cup slivered almonds, toasted
1/8 tsp. white pepper
Salt to taste

Preheat oven to 400 degrees. Wash squash and place whole on oven rack. Bake for 17 to 19 minutes (can be tested for tenderness by piercing with fork). Allow to cool slightly, cut in half, and discard seeds. Scoop out flesh, being careful not to break shells. Press flesh through food processor to puree, or use electric food processor. Mix with butter or margarine and add salt and pepper to taste. Spoon back into shells, mounding the mixture slightly, and stud with almonds. Bake for a few minutes to reheat before serving.

ZUCCHINI CHEESE PUFF

Serves 6

6 medium zucchinis, cut into large chunks
1 cup cottage cheese
1 cup Monterey Jack cheese, shredded
2 eggs, beaten
3/4 tsp. dill weed
1/2 cup soft bread crumbs
1 tbsp. butter, melted

Preheat oven to 350 degrees. Simmer zucchini in salted water for 5 minutes. Drain, and mix with remaining ingredients in shallow 1 1/2 qt. casserole. Bake, uncovered, for 15 minutes. Sprinkle with bread crumbs tossed with melted butter and bake for an additional 15 minutes.

NOODLE AND SPINACH CASSEROLE

Serves 8-10

8 oz. medium-width noodles
Two 10-oz. packages frozen chopped spinach
2 onions
1/2 cup margarine
3 eggs, well beaten
1 cup cottage cheese
1 cup Swiss cheese, grated
Pinch of nutmeg
Salt and pepper to taste

Thaw spinach, press out and discard liquid. Preheat oven to 350 degrees. Boil noodles until tender and drain. Saute onions in margarine, add spinach, mix, then add remaining ingredients and mix again. Place in buttered casserole, cover, and bake for 30 minutes. Uncover and bake for additional 15 minutes.

EGGPLANT CAPONATA

Serves 12-14

1 eggplant, peeled, cut into cubes
1 onion
Olive oil, enough to saute vegetables
1 green pepper, sliced
2 stalks celery, sliced
One 8-oz. can tomato sauce
Salt, pepper, dried basil, and oregano leaves to taste
1 clove garlic, minced
1/2 cup pitted black olives, drained
2 tbsp. capers (optional)

Saute onion in olive oil in covered pan, then add green pepper, eggplant, and celery. Cook for additional 20 minutes. Add tomato paste, sprinkle with basil and oregano leaves, salt, and pepper. Add garlic and olives. Serve at room temperature with crackers.

MUSHROOM SALAD

Serves 4-6

1 lb. small (button) mushrooms, washed
6 tbsp. olive oil
Juice of 2 lemons
3/4-1 tsp. thyme
2 cloves garlic, finely chopped
8 tbsp. parsley, chopped
Salt and pepper to taste

Combine oil, lemon juice, thyme, garlic, and parsley. Mix well, then add salt and pepper and pour over mushrooms. Refrigerate for one day before serving.

FRESH SPINACH SALAD

Serves 6

1 bunch spinach, torn into bite-size pieces
2 cups bean sprouts
1 cup mushrooms, sliced

Toss vegetables together.

Dressing
1/2 cup oil
1/3 cup sugar
1/3 cup wine vinegar
1 onion, chopped fine
Salt and pepper to taste

Combine ingredients, mix until smooth, and refrigerate for at least one day. Pour over vegetables to serve.

CHEESECAKE

Crust

1 cup all-purpose flour (unsifted)
1/2 cup sugar
3 tbsp. cocoa
1 tsp. baking powder
1/8 tsp. salt
1/4 lb. (1/2 cup) soft butter or margarine
1/2 cup walnuts, chopped fine
1 egg yolk (save white for filling)
1 tsp. vanilla

Line bottom and sides of 9-inch-square baking pan with aluminum foil and preheat oven to 325 degrees. Mix flour, sugar, cocoa, baking powder, and salt. Cut butter into mixture, using a pastry blender or two table knives, until it forms pea-size pieces. Add walnuts, egg yolk, and vanilla, and mix well. Press firmly over bottom of baking pan and bake for 15 minutes.

Filling

1 pkg. (8 oz.) cream cheese, room temperature
1/3 cup sugar
1/2 cup sour cream
1 whole egg
1 egg white
1 tbsp. flour
1/4 tsp. salt
2 tsp. grated orange peel
1/2 tsp. vanilla

Combine ingredients in large mixing bowl and beat until well blended. Remove baked crust from oven, pour in filling, and bake until set (20-25 minutes). Leave in pan to cool for about an hour, then garnish top with chocolate chips or chopped almonds, walnuts, or dried fruit.

GRAHAM CRACKER CHEESECAKE

Serves 8-10

Crust

26 to 30 graham crackers or 1 1/4 to
*   1 1/2 cups graham cracker crumbs*
1/2 cube (4 tbsp.) butter, melted or 1/4
*   cup Crisco oil*
1/4 cup sugar

Combine ingredients, mix well, and spread evenly over bottom and sides of baking pan. Preheat oven to 375 degrees.

Filling

18 oz. softened cream cheese
3/4 cup sugar
3 eggs, well beaten
1 tbsp. lemon juice
1/2 pint (1 cup) sour cream
Additional 2 tbsp. sugar
1 tsp. vanilla

Mix together cream cheese and 3/4 cup sugar, add eggs and lemon juice, mix until smooth, and pour into crust. Bake until firm in center (20-30 minutes – do not overcook). Remove from oven and let stand for 15 minutes. Increase oven temperature to 475 degrees. Mix together sour cream, two tbsp. sugar, and one tsp. vanilla. Spread mixture over top of cake and bake for five minutes. Place on rack, allow to cool, and refrigerate overnight.

FRESH FRUIT TORTE

Serves 6-8

Shell
1 1/2 cups all-purpose flour
1/3 cup sugar
1 tsp. lemon rind, grated
1/4 tsp. salt
1/2 tsp. baking powder
1/2 cup butter or margarine
1 egg

Combine flour, sugar, lemon rind, salt, and baking powder in medium size mixing bowl. Add butter or margarine, mix with pastry blender until crumbly, and stir in the egg. Spread evenly over bottom and up the sides of a 9-in. pie plate. Preheat oven to 400 degrees.

Filling
5 cups apples, peeled, thinly sliced
One 16-oz. can sliced peaches, drained
1/2 cup powdered sugar
2 tbsp. brown sugar

Arrange apples and peaches in pie shell so that they overlap slightly. Sprinkle with the powdered sugar and bake for 12 minutes, then sprinkle with the brown sugar. Test apples by piercing with point of paring knife. If they are not tender, bake for additional two to four minutes. Allow to cool, but do not refrigerate.

NUT BREAD

Serves 8-10

3 eggs
1/3 cup oil
3/4 cup sugar
1 cup flour
1 tsp. potato starch
1/2-3/4 cup nuts, chopped
Rind of 1 orange or lemon

Preheat oven to 375 degrees. Combine ingredients and mix well. Pour into greased loaf pan and bake for 25 to 35 minutes.

MONDELBROT

Makes about 60 cookies

3 eggs
3/4 cup sugar
3/4 cup vegetable oil
1 tsp. vanilla
Juice and rind of 1/2 lemon
Dash of salt
3/4 cup brown sugar
3 1/2 to 4 cups flour
1 tsp. baking powder
1/2 tsp. baking soda
1 tsp. cinnamon
1 cup nuts, chopped

Preheat oven to 350 degrees. Beat eggs while slowly adding sugar. Continue to beat and add oil, vanilla, lemon juice and rind, and salt. Mix together flour, baking powder, baking soda, and cinnamon. Continue to beat the egg mixture, slowly add the flour mixture, then the nuts. Roll dough into three or four long loaves and place on greased cookie sheets, two loaves per sheet. Bake for about 30 minutes, then remove from oven, slice diagonally into 1/2-in.-wide segments, lay the slices flat, and continue to bake until brown.

CHAPTER 12

Tu Be Av
(Av 15: August)

And the people were sorry for [the tribe of] Benjamin, because the Lord had made a breach in the tribes of Israel. Then the elders of the community said, "What shall we do to provide wives for those who survived, seeing that the women of Benjamin have been destroyed? . . . We may not give them our daughters in marriage, for the Israelites have sworn an oath, saying cursed be he who gives a wife to Benjamin." Then they said, "However, there is a feast of the Lord in Shiloh every year. . . ." Therefore, they told the Benjaminites, "Go and lie in wait in the vineyards; keep watch. When the daughters of Shiloh come out in groups to dance together, you come out of the vineyards, and each one of you catch a wife from among the daughters of Shiloh, and go to the land of Benjamin. . . ." And the children of Benjamin did so.

Judges 21:15-23

Tu Be Av is a celebration of love and courting. In the days of the Second Temple, Jewish maidens would dress in white and dance in the vineyards. Young men would conceal themselves nearby, then figuratively or literally pounce on the girls and take them for wives. The girls all wore white to make it difficult for the boys to tell which ones had rich fathers.

Even though the Talmud decribes Tu Be Av as one of the most festive holidays, its origin is clouded in mystery. Perhaps it can be traced to the reuniting of the Israelites after the war between the Benjaminites and other tribes. Because of the decimation of the tribe of Benjamin in the war, including the women, the Israelite elders invited the Benjaminite men who had survived to find wives for themselves when the girls of Shiloh went out to dance in the fields. They were to hide in the vineyards, catch as many girls as there were men, and take them back to the land of Benjamin. Or the holiday may commemorate the end of prohibitions against intermarriage between the tribes.

After the destruction of the Temple, the ardent courting rite disappeared. The pioneers who came to Israel in the nineteenth century revived it, but in a more congenial form, and it is still observed in the kibutzim and villages. On Tu Be Av the young women hide in the fields, and the men search for them. The first girl a man finds is his date for a dance held in the moonlight that night. Many a marriage proposal has been made after the dance.

While it might not be practical for the rest of us to play hide-and-seek in the fields just to get a date for the evening, Tu Be Av is a great occasion for an intimate dinner for one or two couples. Appropriate colors are red and pink (suggesting love and affection), white (for the clothes worn by the dancing maidens), and purple or green (for the grapes in the vineyards).

MENU

No ceremony or particular foods are associated with Tu Be Av. But a celebration of love does call for dishes that are a little more exotic than what we usually serve.

Tomatoes with cucumber stuffing, or tomatoes
with artichoke/cucumber stuffing, or sliced tomatoes with
oil and vinegar, or marinated peppers, or red cabbage salad
Rolled chicken breast, or cornish game hens, or chicken in wine,
or chicken with artichokes, or cherry chicken or
sweet and sour chicken
Rice pilaf, or rice and lentils
Strawberry fluff, or chocolate mousse, or berry salad

TABLE DECORATION

Hearts express the theme of a Tu Be Av dinner, of course. For a simple table decoration, use hearts as napkin rings (either plastic ones obtainable with elastic bands in many gift stores, or cut them out of red wrapping paper and lay them over the napkins). A basket of grapes is ample for a centerpiece. If your guests don't know what the grapes mean, you can have fun telling them about the ancient methods of courtship. Dress up the table a bit more with a pair of dice – representing the gamble of falling in love – small baskets of grapes, and artificial grape leaves as coasters. Use a pink tablecloth and purple napkins, or vice versa.

Following are some alternative ideas for thematic tables:

LOVE POEMS.   Cover the table with hearts cut out of red, pink, purple, and white wrapping or crepe paper, and write on them quotations from the Song of Songs or your favorite love poems. For a centerpiece, place grapes around a large red heart – perhaps a heart-shaped box, if you have one. Next to each place setting, put a pink or red candle and a love poem – you can photocopy ones in books on pink or red paper. Eat by candlelight.

DANCING IN THE VINEYARD.   Stress the color white – the tablecloth, napkins, and the candles (preferably with white or glass holders.) Add color by using artificial grape leaves as coasters for the candles and by placing a small basket of grapes at each place setting. For the centerpiece use figurines of dancers, if you have them, or a doll dressed in white. On each napkin place a key (to the guest's heart).

CINDERELLA.   Stress the color pink with your tablecloth and napkins. For a centerpiece make a garland – or just a circle – out of pink flowers, and in the middle place a cinderella slipper, which you can obtain in shops that sell costumes or some paper-goods stores. If you can't find one, just use an evening-wear shoe. Surround the garland with chunky white candles. At each place setting put a paper or plastic miniature shoe (obtainable in paper-goods stores), and place red flowers, purple grapes, or candy kisses in the shoe.

GIFTS FOR THE HOST

Book of love poems
Box of candy, or chocolate kisses
Champagne
Cosmetics
Gift certificate for a beauty shop or health spa
Grapes in a basket
Jewelry box
Picture frame, heart-shaped
Recording of love song(s)
Tickets for a show

MEMENTOS FOR GUESTS

Button, campaign-type with appropriate slogan, such
    as "make love not war"
Flower, red or pink (preferably a rose)
Grape jam, jar
Wine, small bottle

SUMMARY OF ORNAMENTS

Candles
Cinderella slipper
Dice
Doll dress in white
Figurines of dancers
Garland (or circle) of flowers
Grape leaves, artificial, as coasters
Grapes
Hearts (plastic, cut outs, boxes)
Keys
Love poems
Quotations from Song of Songs and/or love poems
Shoes (miniature)

RECIPES

TOMATOES WITH CUCUMBER STUFFING

Serves 6

6 large firm tomatoes
4 large cucumbers, peeled, thinly sliced
1 scallion, diced
1 tsp. salt
1/2 tsp. sugar
2 tbsp. lemon juice
3 tbsp. olive oil
Black pepper to taste

Place cucumbers and scallion in a bowl. Mix together salt, sugar, lemon juice, and olive oil. Add pepper to mixture and pour over scallion and cucumbers. Mix, and refrigerate for at least two hours. (Can be made up to a day in advance.) Wash tomatoes and dry. Cut off top third of each and save. Scoop insides out of tomatoes, stuff with cucumber mixture, and cover with tomato tops. Garnish with parsley and serve on lettuce leaves.

TOMATOES WITH
ARTICHOKE/CUCUMBER STUFFING

Serves 4

4 large ripe tomatoes
1 large cucumber, peeled, cut into small chunks
1/2 tsp. fresh cilantro, chopped
6 pitted black olives, chopped
4 pitted green olives, chopped
1 jar (6 oz.) artichoke hearts, drained, chopped
Salt and pepper to taste
1 tbsp. lemon juice
2 tbsp. olive oil

Cut tops off tomatoes and hollow out insides, leaving 1/4-1/2-inch-thick shells. Drain over paper towels. Chop firm flesh and mix with cucumber, cilantro, olives, artichoke hearts, salt, and pepper. Mix lemon juice and olive oil, pour over salad, mix well, then stuff heaping portions into tomato shells. Serve each portion on top of butter lettuce leaves.

MARINATED PEPPERS

Serves 6-8

1 large red pepper, cut into strips
1 large yellow pepper, cut into strips
2 large green peppers, cut into strips
1 large onion, cut and separated into rings
1/4 cup olive oil
1/4 cup white vinegar
Salt and pepper to taste
2 tbsp. fresh basil or parsley

Heat oil in pan, add peppers and onion, cover, and cook for about five minutes. Transfer to salad bowl, add the white vinegar, salt, and pepper. Refrigerate for a few hours. Before serving, sprinkle with fresh basil or parsley.

RED CABBAGE SALAD

Serves 4-6

1 medium-size red cabbage
1/2 cup water
1/4 cup vinegar
1 tbsp. sugar
1/2 cup oil
1/2 cup chopped parsley
1/4 cup chopped walnut
Salt and pepper to taste

Finely shred cabbage. Mix water, vinegar, and sugar, bring to boil, and pour over cabbage. Cover, and keep at room temperature for about five hours. Mix oil, parsley, walnuts, salt, and pepper, add to cabbage, and toss.

ROLLED CHICKEN BREAST

8 chicken breast halves, boned, skinned
3 tbsp. margarine
8 medium mushrooms, chopped
1/4 cup walnuts, chopped
1/4 cup pistachios, chopped
1/4 cup broccoli, chopped
1/4 cup soft bread crumbs
1/4 cup steamed rice
1/4 tsp. salt
1/8 tsp. pepper
1/4 tsp. paprika
1 orange, sliced
Parsley

White Wine Sauce
2 tsp. cornstarch
1/2 cup dry white wine
1/4 cup margarine, melted
1/2 cup apricot preserves

Mix wine and cornstarch in small saucepan. Stir until smooth, then continue to stir while adding margarine and apricot preserves. Cook over medium low heat until mixture is translucent. Sprinkle chicken with paprika, salt, and pepper, then lightly pound each breast to an even thickness. Preheat oven to 350 degrees. Melt three tbsp. margarine in a small skillet. Add mushrooms, pistachios, walnuts, and broccoli. Saute until mushrooms are tender, then stir in bread crumbs and rice. Spread a spoonful of the mixture across the center of each breast, roll up (jelly roll style), and secure with wooden picks. Place rolls in baking pan, spoon wine sauce over them, and bake until tender (30-40 minutes). Spoon any remaining sauce over the baked rolls after arranging them on a serving plate. Decorate with orange slices and garnish with sprigs of parsley.

CORNISH GAME HENS

Serves 10-12

6 cornish hens, about 1 1/4 lb. each
1/4 tsp. salt
1/8 tsp. pepper
2 tbsp. dried tarragon leaves
1/2 clove garlic, chopped fine
3/4 cup margarine, melted
3/4 cup dry white wine
Additional salt and pepper to taste
Garlic salt

Thaw hens completely, if frozen. Preheat oven to 450 degrees. Rinse hens and wipe dry. Mix together salt, pepper, one tbsp. dried tarragon leaves, and garlic, and sprinkle into cavity of each hen. Mix together margarine, wine, and remaining tarragon leaves to make basting sauce, add salt and pepper to taste, and brush over hens. Sprinkle hens with garlic salt, tie feet together, and place in large baking pan. Bake for one hour or until golden brown and tender, basting and turning over once every 20 minutes.

CHICKEN IN WINE
(Also see Chapter 7, Purim.)

Serves 4-6

One 3-lb. chicken, cut up
2 tbsp. oil
2 tbsp. vegetable margarine, melted
1 large onion, chopped, sauted in 2 tbsp. oil
3/4 cup dry red wine
1 cup mushrooms, sliced

Mix together oil and margarine in skillet. Dip chicken pieces in flour and brown over high heat in oil-margarine mixture. Add onion, wine, and mushrooms. Cook over low heat until chicken is tender (20-30 minutes). If sauce is too thin when chicken is ready, thicken with one tsp. flour or 1/2 tsp. cornstarch.

CHICKEN WITH ARTICHOKES

(Also see Chapter 4, Sukkoth and Simchas Torah.)   Serves 4

4 half-breasts of chicken
3/4 tsp. seasoned salt
One 6-oz. jar marinated artichokes, drained (reserve juice)
1 tbsp. flour
1/2 cup water
1/4 cup dry white wine
1 cube chicken bouillon, crushed
14 small mushrooms, cut in half
1 tbsp. parsley, chopped
Pepper to taste

Pat salt onto chicken breasts, brown in three tbsp. artichoke marinade, and remove from pan. Leave one tbsp. of marinade in the pan, add flour, mix, then add water, wine, and bouillon. Bring to boil, continuing to mix. When sauce has thickened, arrange chicken breasts in pan, place artichokes and mushrooms on top, and pour in remaining marinade. Cover, and cook over low heat for 15 minutes. Sprinkle with parsley before serving.

CHERRY CHICKEN

Serves 6-8

Two 3-lb. chickens, cut up
1/2 cup brown sugar
One 12-oz. bottle chile sauce
2 tsp. minced onion
One 1-lb. can pitted dark cherries, drained
1/2 cup cream sherry wine

Preheat oven to 400 degrees. Put chicken in deep baking dish and place in oven to brown. Combine remaining ingredients, bring to boil, and pour over chicken. Cover baking dish, lower heat to 350 degrees, and bake for one hour or until chicken is tender.

SWEET N' SOUR CHICKEN

Serves 6-8

Two 3-lb. chickens, cut up
One 15- or 16-oz. can pineapple chunks,
drained (save juice)
1/3 cup vinegar
2 tbsp. cornstarch
1/2 cup brown sugar
2 tbsp. soy sauce
1 green pepper, cut into strips

Fry chicken until golden brown. Pour pineapple juice, vinegar, cornstarch, brown sugar, and soy sauce into a large saucepan and stir until well mixed. Add pineapple and green pepper. Cook over medium heat for five minutes, stirring frequently. Fold in chicken pieces, lower heat, and cook for 45 to 60 minutes.

RICE PILAF

Serves 4-6

3 cups chicken broth
1 1/2 cups long-grain rice, uncooked
4 tbsp. oil
1/4 cup raisins
1/2 tsp. tumeric
1/2 tsp. sherry
1 1/2 tsp. soy sauce

Bring broth to boil, then add remaining ingredients. Cook over low heat for 25 to 30 minutes. Fluff with fork and serve.

RICE WITH LENTILS

Serves 4-6

1 onion, chopped
Two 10 1/2-oz. cans chicken broth
3/4 cup rice
1/2 cup lentils
1/2 tsp. salt
1/8 tsp. pepper

Saute onion, then add chicken broth, salt, and pepper. Bring to boil, add remaining ingredients, lower heat, and cook for 30 to 35 minutes. Stir lightly and serve.

CHOCOLATE MOUSSE

Serves 6-8

8 oz. bittersweet chocolate, broken into pieces
6 tbsp. strong hot coffee
5 eggs, separated
1 tbsp. wine or any type of spirits desired

Place chocolate and coffee in double boiler or microwave dish and melt chocolate. Allow to cool, meanwhile beat egg whites until they form stiff peaks. Beat yolks and add to cooled chocolate. Fold in egg whites and add wine. Spoon into crystal glasses and chill, or spoon into cupcake papers and freeze. Leave in refrigerator or freezer until time to serve. To add flavor and elegant appearance, serve with fresh strawberry on top.

BERRY SALAD

Serves 6-8

1/4 lb. raspberries
1/4 lb. blueberries
1/4 lb. boysenberries
1/4 lb. strawberries, sliced
1/4 lb. grapes, seedless
1/4 lb. almonds, finely chopped

Place ingredients in large bowl and stir very gently, taking care not to bruise the berries, until all varieties are evenly distributed. Serve in small bowls.

STRAWBERRY FLUFF

Serves 4-6

2 egg whites
1 cup sugar
1 1/2 cups fresh strawberries, mashed
1 tbsp. fresh lemon juice

Beat egg whites until stiff. Continue beating at high speed while gradually adding sugar, then lemon juice. Add strawberries and beat until stiff. Spoon into crystal glasses or cupcake papers and freeze. Place two tbsp. salad oil and a 50-gram bittersweet chocolate bar in double boiler and melt chocolate. Dip frozen fluffs in chocolate, or spoon chocolate over tops, to form coating. (The chocolate hardens immediately.) Put back into freezer until time to serve.

A Selection of Jewish Holiday Songs

SHALOM ALĒḤEM (Peace unto You)

SABBATH

I. & S.E. Goldfarb

Peace unto you, O angels of peace. May your coming

be in peace, and your going forth.

SHABBAT HAMALKA (Sabbath Queen)

SABBATH

Heb. verse: H.N.Bialik
Eng. verse: A.I.Cohon

Music: F.Minkowsky

Ha - ha - ma më - rosh ha - i - la not nis - tal - ka, Bo -
u v' - në - tse lik - rat sha - bat ha - mal - ka. Hi - në hi yo -
re - det hak' - do - sha hab' - ru - ha. V' - i - ma mal - a - him ts'va -
sha - lom um' - nu - ha. Bo - i, bo - i, ha - mal - - -
ka, bo - i, bo - i, ha - ka - la. Sha -
lom a - lë - hem mal - a - hë ha sha - lom.

The sun on the tree-tops no long - er is seen!__ Come
gath - er to wel - come the Sab - bath, our queen.__ Be - hold her de -
scend - ing, the ho - ly, the blest.__ And with her the an - gels of
peace and of rest. Draw near, O Queen and here __ a -
bide, draw near, draw near, O Sab - bath bride. And
peace __ to you, __ ye an - gels of __ peace.

We've welcomed the Sabbath with song and with prayer:
And home we return our heart's gladness to share.
The table is set and the candles are lit.
The tiniest corner for Sabbath made fit.
O day of blessing, day or rest!
Sweet day of peace be ever blest!
Bring ye also peace, ye angels of peace!

V'AL KULAM
(O Lord of Forgiveness)

ROSH HASHANAH

Liturgy

Traditional

O Lord of forgiveness, forgive us for all our sins.

וְעַל כֻּלָּם אֱלוֹהַּ סְלִיחוֹת
סְלַח לָנוּ, מְחַל לָנוּ, כַּפֶּר־לָנוּ.

ENTERTAINING ON THE JEWISH HOLIDAYS

KOL NIDRË (All Vows)

YOM KIPPUR

Liturgy

Traditional

Slowly, with feeling

Kol nid - rë ___ ve - e - sa - rë ___ v'-ha - ra -
më ___ v'-ko - na - më ___ v'-hi - nu - yë ___ v' - ki - nu -
së ___ u - sh'-vu - ot. Din ___ - dar - na u - d' - ish ___ - t'-
va - na u - d'-a ___ - ha - rim - na. V'-
di - a - sar - na ___ al ___ naf - sha - ta - na. ___

All vows, oaths and promises to God with which we
have bound ourselves shall be nullified.

כָּל נִדְרֵי וֶאֱסָרֵי וּשְׁבוּעֵי וַחֲרָמֵי
וְקוֹנָמֵי וּקְנָסֵי וְכִנּוּיֵי
דְּאִנְדַּרְנָא וּדְאִשְׁתַּבַּעְנָא וּדְאַחֲרִימְנָא
וּדְאָסַרְנָא עַל נַפְשָׁתָנָא.

HASUKA MA YAFA (Lovely Is the Sukkah) **SUKKOTH**

Text by H.C.

Folk song
Second part: H.C.

Joyously

Ha - su - ka   ma   ya - fa,   u - ma   tov   la -

she-vet ba. ___   she-vet ba.   La la la la   la la la

u - ma   tov   la - she-vet ba.   la - she-vet   ba.

3) *Ha-suka ma na'a*
   U-ma tov le-e-ḥol ba.
   La-la-la – – –

4) *No-de lo, no-de lo*
   Ki l'o-lam ḥas-do.
   La-la-la – – –

How lovely is the Sukkah!
To enter it is a delight.
Welcome! How nice it is
to eat in it. Let's thank our
God for he is always gracious.

הַסֻּכָּה מָה נָאָה
וּמַה טוֹב לֶאֱכֹל בָּה.
לַ – לַ – לַ...
וּמַה טוֹב לֶאֱכֹל בָּה.

נוֹדֶה לוֹ, נוֹדֶה לוֹ
כִּי לְעוֹלָם חַסְדּוֹ.
לַ – לַ – לַ...
כִּי לְעוֹלָם חַסְדּוֹ.

הַסֻּכָּה מָה יָפָה
וּמַה טוֹב לָשֶׁבֶת בָּה.
לַ – לַ – לַ...
וּמַה טוֹב לָשֶׁבֶת בָּה.

בָּרוּךְ הַבָּא, בָּרוּךְ הַבָּא
הִכָּנֵס בְּבַקָּשָׁה,
לַ – לַ – לַ...
הִכָּנֵס בְּבַקָּשָׁה.

SIMHAT TORAH
(Joy of the Torah)

SIMHATH TORAH

Liturgy

Ḥasidic

Si - su v'-sim-ḥu __ b'-sim-ḥat to - rah ut'-

nu __ ka - vod __ la-to - rah, ___ ki tov __ saḥ -

ra - mi - kol s'ho - ra mi - paz u-mi p'ni-nim __ y'-ka -

ra. Na - gil __ v'-na-sis, na - gil __ v'-na-sis b'-

zot __ ha-to-rah, __ ha-to - rah, ___ ki hi __ la-nu oz, ki

hi __ la-nu oz, oz, oz v'-o - ra. Si -

D.S. al FINE

Let us rejoice with our Torah.
It is our strength and our light.

מִפָּז וּמִפְּנִינִים יְקָרָה.
נָגִיל וְנָשִׂישׂ בְּזֹאת הַתּוֹרָה,
כִּי הִיא לָנוּ עֹז וְאוֹרָה.

שִׂישׂוּ וְשִׂמְחוּ בְּשִׂמְחַת תּוֹרָה,
וּתְנוּ כָבוֹד לַתּוֹרָה,
כִּי טוֹב סַחְרָה
מִכָּל סְחוֹרָה.

SIMHATH TORAH

HAL'LU SHABḤU SH'MU
(Praise His Name)

Liturgy

Music: J. Grossman

We praise the Lord in His holiness, and praise
Him in His mighty firmament.

הַלְלוּ שַׁבְּחוּ שְׁמוֹ, שְׂמְחוּ וְהוֹדוּ לוֹ.
הַלְלוּיָהּ, הַלְלוּיָהּ, הַלְלוּיָהּ, הַלְלוּיָהּ,
הַלְלוּיָהּ, הַלְלוּ, הַלְלוּיָהּ.

MI Y'MALËL (Who Can Retell?)

HANUKKAH

English verse: B.M.Edidin

Music adapted by M.Ravina

Rhythmically

Mi y'-ma-lël g'vu - rot yis-ra-ël? O - tan mi yim - ne?
Who can re-tell the things that be-fell us? Who can count them?

Hën b'-ḥol dor ya - kum ha-gi-bor go - ël ha - am.
In ev- ery age a he-ro or sage came to our aid.

Sh'ma! Ba - ya - mim ha - hëm baz'-man ha - ze,
Hark! In days of yore, in Is-rael's an-cient land, Brave

ma - ka-bi mo-shi-a u-fo - de, uv' ya-më - nu kol am yis-ra-
Mac-ca-be- us led the faith-ful band. But now all Is-rael must as one a-

ël, yit'-a-hëd ya-kum l'-hi-ga - ël.
rise, Re - deem it-self thru deed and sac-ri - fice.

שְׁמַע! בַּיָּמִים הָהֶם בַּזְּמַן הַזֶּה
מַכַּבִּי מוֹשִׁיעַ וּפוֹדֶה.
וּבְיָמֵינוּ כָּל עַם יִשְׂרָאֵל
יִתְאַחֵד יָקוּם לְהִגָּאֵל!

מִי יְמַלֵּל גְּבוּרוֹת יִשְׂרָאֵל?
(* מִי יְמַלֵּל גְּבוּרוֹת יְיָ)
אוֹתָן מִי יִמְנֶה?
הֵן בְּכָל דּוֹר יָקוּם הַגִּבּוֹר,
גּוֹאֵל הָעָם.

HOLIDAY SONGS

157

HASHKĖDIYA (Tu Be Shevat Is Here)

TU BE SHEVAT

Lyrics: M. Dushman
Eng. lyrics: S. Dinin

Music: M. Ravina

Hash - kë - di - ya po - ra - ḥat, v' - she-mesh paz zo - ra - ḥat
The al-mond tree is grow-ing, a gold-en sun is glow-ing;

tsi - pa - rim më - rosh kol gag m' - vas-rot et bo he-ḥag.
The birds sing out in joy-ous glee from ev-ery roof and ev-ery tree.

Tu bish'-vat hi - gi - a, ḥag ha - i - la - not,
Tu Bish-vat is here, _____ the Jew-ish Ar - bor Day,

Tu bish'-vat hi - gi - a, ḥag ha - i - la - not.
Hail the trees' New Year, _____ Hap-py ho - li - day!

Ha-a-retz m'sha-va-at:	הָאָרֶץ מְשַׁוַּעַת:
Hi-gi-a ët la-ta-at.	הִגִּיעָה עֵת לָטַעַת.
Kol e-ḥad yi-kaḥ lo ëtz,	כָּל אֶחָד יַקַּח לוֹ עֵץ,
Ba-i-tim në-tzë ho-tzëtz:	בָּאתִים נֵצֵא חוֹצֵץ:
Tu bi-Sh'vat...	ט״ו בִּשְׁבָט...

Ni-ta kol har va-ge-va	נִטַּע כָּל הַר וָגֶבַע
Mi-Dan v'ad B'ër She-va.	מִדָּן וְעַד בְּאֵר שֶׁבַע.
V'ar-tzë-nu shuv ni-rash	וְאַרְצֵנוּ שׁוּב נִירַשׁ
E-retz za-yit, ḥa-lav u-d'vash.	אֶרֶץ זַיִת, חָלָב וּדְבַשׁ.
Tu bi-Sh'vat...	ט״ו בִּשְׁבָט...

הַשְּׁקֵדִיָּה פּוֹרַחַת,
וְשֶׁמֶשׁ פָּז זוֹרַחַת.
צִפֳּרִים מֵרֹאשׁ כָּל גַּג
מְבַשְׂרוֹת אֶת בֹּא הֶחָג:
ט״ו בִּשְׁבָט הִגִּיעַ –
חַג הָאִילָנוֹת.

Let's make the land a garden,
With water from the Jordan;
And our land will flow once more
With milk and honey, as of yore.

Chorus

UTSU ËTSA (They Scheme and Plot)

U-tsu ë-tsa v'-tu - far, u-tsu ë-tsa v'-tu -
far, u-tsu ë-tsa v'-tu-far,— dab-ru da-var v'-lo ya-kum,
ki__ i-ma-nu__ ël, __ u-tsu ë-tsa v'-tu-far,
dab-ru da-var v'-lo ya-kum, ki__ i-ma-nu__ ël.
U-tsu ë-tsa v'-tu - far, dab-ru da-var v'-lo ya -
kum, u-tsu ë-tsa v'-tu-far,— dab-ru da-var v'-lo ya-kum,
ki__ i-ma-nu__ ël, __ u-tsu ë-tsa v'-tu-far,
dab-ru da-var v'-lo ya-kum, ki__ i-ma-nu__ ël.

They may scheme and plot against us,
but to no avail; for God is always with us.

עוּצוּ עֵצָה וְתוּפָר,
דַּבְּרוּ דָבָר וְלֹא יָקוּם,
כִּי עִמָּנוּ אֵל.

159

ADIR HU (Mighty Is He)

Hagada

Traditional

Ba-ḥur hu, ga-dol hu.	בָּחוּר הוּא, גָּדוֹל הוּא.	אַדִּיר הוּא, אַדִּיר הוּא.
yivne...	יבנה...	יִבְנֶה בֵיתוֹ בְּקָרוֹב.
Da-gul hu, ha-dur hu.	דָּגוּל הוּא, הָדוּר הוּא.	בִּמְהֵרָה, בִּמְהֵרָה,
yivne...	יבנה...	בְּיָמֵינוּ בְּקָרוֹב.
Va-tik hu, za-kai hu.	וָתִיק הוּא, זַכַּאי הוּא.	אֵל בְּנֵה, אֵל בְּנֵה
yivne...	יבנה..	בְּנֵה בֵיתְךָ בְּקָרוֹב.

Father, we pray to Thee,
   Let Thy grace be o'er us;
Let Thy light, and Thy might
   Show the paths before us;
Ours Thy love, from above,
   And Thy grace which bore us.

Lo! The spring joy doth bring,
   Winter's frosts are ended;
Gladness reigns, life remains,
   With sweet pleasure blended;
God doth bear what His care
   And His love defended.

L'SHANA HABA'A (Next Year)

PASSOVER

Hagada

Music: M. Nathanson

L'-sha-na ha-ba-a, l'-sha-na ha-ba-a,

l'-sha-na ha-ba-a ____ bi y'-ru-sha-la-yim.

L'- sha-na _____ ha-ba-a, _____ l'- sha-

na ha-ba-a bi-y'-ru-sha-la-yim. L'-sha-na ha-ba-a,

l'-sha-na ha-ba-a, biy'-ru-sha-la - yim.

Next year may we be in Jerusalem.

לְשָׁנָה הַבָּאָה בִּירוּשָׁלַיִם.

HATIKVA (The Hope)

YOM HA'ATZMAUT
(Israeli Independence Day)

Verse: N.Imber

Kol _ od ba-lĕ-vav p'ni - ma ne - fesh ye hu - di ho - mi - ya, u - l'-fa'a-te _ miz - raḥ ka - di - ma a - yin l'-tsi - yon tso - fi - ya. Od lo av - da tik-va-tĕ - nu, ha - tik - va sh'not al-pa - yim, lih' - yot am ḥaf - shi b' - ar - tsĕ - nu e - rets _ tsi - yon viy' - ru-sha-la - yim.

כָּל עוֹד בַּלֵּבָב פְּנִימָה
נֶפֶשׁ יְהוּדִי הוֹמִיָּה,
וּלְפַאֲתֵי מִזְרָח קָדִימָה
עַיִן לְצִיּוֹן צוֹפִיָּה.

עוֹד לֹא אָבְדָה תִקְוָתֵנוּ,
הַתִּקְוָה שְׁנוֹת אַלְפַּיִם,
לִהְיוֹת עַם חָפְשִׁי בְּאַרְצֵנוּ,
בְּאֶרֶץ צִיּוֹן וִירוּשָׁלַיִם.

So long as the heart of the Jew beats and his
eye is turned to the East, so long does our ancient
hope of returning to Zion still live.

ENTERTAINING ON THE JEWISH HOLIDAYS

HAYA'A RA (To the Meadow)

LAG BA'OMER

Lyrics: J.Fishman
English: J.I.Sampter

Music: H.Coopersmith

HAYA'A RA (Cont.)

LAG BA'OMER

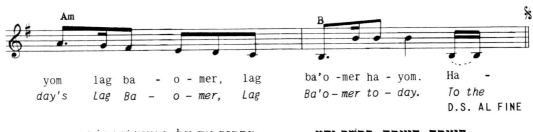

yom   lag   ba - o - mer,   lag   ba'o -mer ha - yom.   Ha -
day's Lag   Ba - o - mer,   Lag   Ba'o-mer to - day.   *To the*
                                                           D.S. AL FINE

מִסָּבִיב אַךְ גִּיל, וּרְנָנִים שָׁם וּפֹה,   הַיַּעֲרָה, הַיַּעֲרָה, בְּקֶשֶׁת וָחֵץ,
הֵעִירוּ בְּנֵי חֹפֶשׁ, הֵרִיעוּ הוּ הוֹ,   נְבוֹאָה שָׂדֶה, שָׁם בֵּין פֶּרַח וָנֵץ,
יָרוּ בַּעֲלֵי חֵץ וְרֹבֶה "פִּי פּוֹ"   שָׁם יֶרֶק וְצִפּוֹר וְרַחַב אֵין קֵץ,
הַיּוֹם לַ"ג בָּעֹמֶר, לַ"ג בָּעֹמֶר הַיּוֹם.   הַיּוֹם לַ"ג בָּעֹמֶר, לַ"ג בָּעֹמֶר הַיּוֹם.

BARUḤ ELOHËNU (Blessed Is Our God)

SHAVUOTH

Liturgy

Ḥasidic
Arr.: H.C.

Ba-ruḥ e-lo-hë - nu she-bra-a - nu liḥ-vo-do, v'- hiv-di-la-nu min-ha-to-im, v'- na-tan la-nu to-rat e - met. met.

Ba-ruḥ e-lo-hë - nu she-bra-a - nu liḥ-vo-do, v'- hiv-di-la-nu min ha-to-im, v'- na-tan la-nu to-rat e - met. met.

Blessed is our God who created us for His glory; who distinguished us from the erring; who gave us the Torah of truth.

בָּרוּךְ אֱלֹהֵינוּ שֶׁבְּרָאָנוּ לִכְבוֹדוֹ,
וְהִבְדִּילָנוּ מִן הַתּוֹעִים, וְנָתַן לָנוּ תּוֹרַת אֱמֶת.

KOL DODI (My Beloved's Voice)

TU BE AV

Song of Songs

Music: H.Coopersmith

Moderately

Kol ___ do - di hi - në ze ba, hi - në ___ ze ___ ba, kol ___

___ do - di hi - në ze ba, hi - në ___ ze ___ ba. M' - da-lëg ___ al
ka-pëts ___ al

he - ha - rim, he - ha - rim, ___ he - ha - rim, m' - ot. Kol ___
ha - g'-va-ot, ha - g'-va-ot, ___ ha - g'-va

D.C. AL FINE

'Hark! my beloved! behold, he cometh,
Leaping upon the mountains, skipping upon the hills.

קוֹל דּוֹדִי הִנֵּה־זֶה בָּא מְדַלֵּג
עַל־הֶהָרִים מְקַפֵּץ עַל־הַגְּבָעוֹת: